William Spiers

Rambles and Reveries of a Naturalist

William Spiers

Rambles and Reveries of a Naturalist

ISBN/EAN: 9783337023973

Printed in Europe, USA, Canada, Australia, Japan

Cover: Foto ©Andreas Hilbeck / pixelio.de

More available books at **www.hansebooks.com**

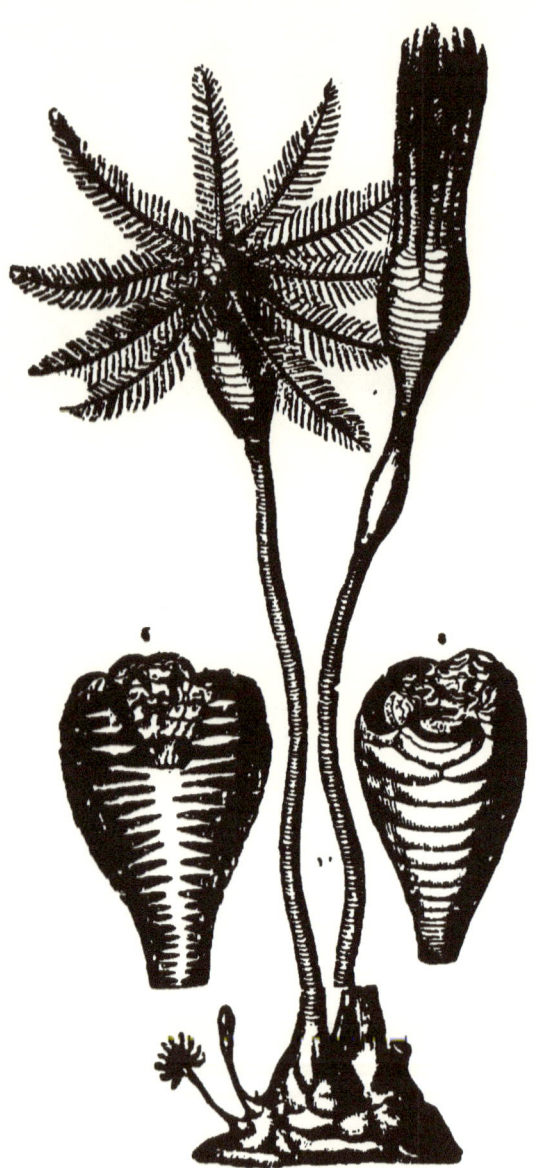

Sea-lily. *Apiocrinus rotundus.*

RAMBLES AND REVERIES

OF A

NATURALIST.

BY THE

REV. WILLIAM SPIERS, M.A.,

F.G.S., F.R.M.S., ETC.,

CO-EDITOR OF THE 'JOURNAL OF MICROSCOPY AND NATURAL SCIENCE.'

LONDON:

CHARLES H. KELLY, 2, CASTLE STREET, CITY ROAD, E.C.;

AND 66, PATERNOSTER ROW, E.C.

1890.

Printed by Hasell, Watson, & Viney, Ld., London and Aylesbury.

PREFACE.

HIS little volume of Natural History sketches has very little to do with opinions or speculations. The aim of the writer has been to describe the facts and phenomena of Nature as they have appeared to present themselves to his own observation. They are life-pictures rather than compilations. So far as systematic arrangement is concerned, there has certainly been an effort to treat each subject taken up in such a way as to lay at least a stepping-stone on the path to a more serious contemplation of the sciences of the text-book and the laboratory, but the primary intention of the author has been rather to awaken or to stimulate a love for Nature in the minds of some who may not as yet have suspected what wondrous and ever-varying beauty lies everywhere about us in ditch and pond, in rock and stone, in river and sea, on earth and in the skies.

The same objects have been described by other and abler pens, but facts and laws present themselves in different aspects to different minds, and the ceaseless and diversified operations of Nature cannot be too frequently portrayed. Even those who would not care to claim the character of students of Nature are not unwilling to be considered lovers of Nature, and for such the plain and non-technical descriptions of a few of her secrets, by those who tell the story of what they themselves have seen and felt in her presence, cannot fail to possess some degree of interest.

As to the value of scientific study in these days, it is almost superfluous to argue. As a means of mental discipline, the methods of inquiry and reasoning made use of in the pursuit of physical science are of great utility, while almost all matters affecting health and life are of such a sort as to be profitably dealt with only by a rigid adherence to those methods. What misery some bring upon themselves and others by dense ignorance of the most elementary laws of Nature ! And certainly the sum of happiness is much increased by some acquaintance, however superficial, with the results of the researches and doctrines of men of science which bear upon the vast problems concerned in the origin and history of life, the development and meaning of organic forms, and the principles upon which the government of the material universe is carried on. In regard to the spirit and aims of such studies, nothing can be more admirable than the following words of Charles Kingsley on this point, in which he sets forth the qualifications of the observer of Nature : "He should be brave and enterprising, and withal patient and undaunted ; not merely in travel, but in investigation ; knowing (as Lord Bacon might have put it) that the Kingdom of Nature, like the Kingdom of Heaven, must be taken by violence, and that only to those who knock long and earnestly does the great mother open the doors of her sanctuary. He must be of a reverent turn of mind also, not rashly discrediting any reports, however vague and fragmentary, giving man credit always for some germ of worth, and giving Nature credit for an inexhaustible fertility and variety, which will keep him his life long always reverent, yet never superstitious ; wondering at the commonest, but not surprised by the most strange ; free from the idols of size and sensuous loveliness ; able to see grandeur in the minutest objects, beauty in the most ungainly ; estimating each thing, not carnally, as the vulgar do, by its size, or its pleasantness to the senses, but

spiritually, by the amount of Divine thought revealed to him therein ; holding every phenomenon
worth the noting down ; believing that every
pebble holds a treasure, every bud a revelation ;
making it a point of conscience to pass over
nothing through laziness or hastiness, lest the
vision, once offered and despised, should be with-
drawn ; and looking at every object as if he
were never to behold it again."— *Glaucus*, p. 46.

This volume is mainly the record of pursuits
which occupied holiday hours snatched from a
life devoted to other and more serious tasks,
but it has often been felt that these pursuits,
while being a relief from the strain of other
kinds of work, have yet been in a large measure
in harmony with it, and helpful to its better
performance. The preaching of the Gospel covers
a wider ground than the mere interpretation of
a written Word. Nature has revelations for man
if he will try to read them intelligently. She
may not be able to answer all the instincts of
his complex being, but she has much to say
that is vitally concerned in his moral, social, and
spiritual welfare. It is the duty of the teacher
of religion, we contend, to seek philosophical and
scientific truth, as well as to expound and enforce
theological doctrines. To leave out of our litera-
ture all that bears upon the exposition of Nature's

processes and marvels is, we think, to betray our
cause, and to show ourselves incapable of grasping
its sacredness and its grandeur, and can only
result in handing over our best and noblest sons,
the flower and hope of the Christian Church, to
influences that may be inimical to their faith
and their devotion to God and humanity. It
is considerations of this kind that have led to
the inclusion of what we prefer to call Reveries
amongst papers which are more properly described
as accounts of Rambles of a Naturalist.

CONTENTS.

LIST OF ILLUSTRATIONS.

I.

AMONGST THE SEAWEEDS.

." Thou sea, who wast to me a prophet deep
  Through all thy restless waves and wasting shores,
· Of silent labour, and eternal change ;
  First teacher of the dense immensity
  Of ever-stirring life, in thy strange forms
  Of fish, and shell, and worm, and oozy weed:
  To me alike thy frenzy and thy sleep
  Have been a deep and breathless joy."

KINGSLEY.

HERE are very few of my readers, pro-
bably, who have not found some degree
of pleasure in collecting seaweeds during
their holidays, even though there has
been no sort of scientific interest in the occupation.
Yet it is quite as entertaining, and assuredly more
profitable, to turn these familiar things to account
in the way of increasing our knowledge of Nature.
To those for whom anything like a practical study
of any branch of natural history is impossible save
during the week or two which, once a year or so,
is snatched from a busy life, a few notes on the
subject of seaweeds, suggested by my own observations and wants, may be of some value. Although

2

during one of my vacations I gave myself up almost exclusively to seaweed collecting, yet my sphere of operations was so limited, and the kind of shore which I worked was so uniform, that I must draw somewhat upon previous experiences as well as upon the results of others' work if I would be of any service.

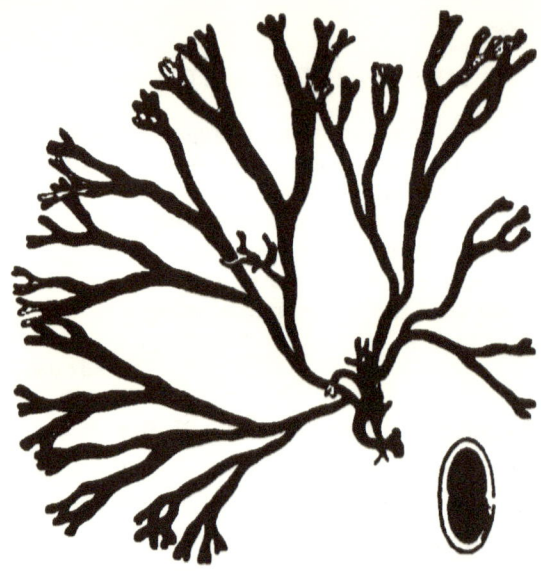

Fig. 1.—*Fucus canaliculatus*, and spore containing sporules.

It may not be amiss, in the first place, to settle what we mean by a seaweed. The very common " grass-wrack," a sort of sea-grass, is not a true seaweed. This plant, which botanists call *Zostera marina*, is really a true flowering plant, whereas seaweeds proper are non-flowering, cellular plants, and constitute the lowest group of the great Linnean division of *Cryptogamia*, to which also belong lichens, fungi, mosses, and ferns. What we are concerned with, then, are marine algæ, plants that have no vascular tissue, nor any root, stem, leaves, flowers, nor seeds. There are seaweeds which seem to possess roots, but these are mere sucker-like discs, and have no root-functions in regard to nutrition, while the so-called stems and leaves are, accurately speaking, fronds and their modifications. Those curious vesicles on so many marine algæ, which look like pods or seed-vessels, and which the novice might suppose were concerned in reproduction, are in reality nothing but air-vessels, whose function is to keep the fronds floating. The higher algæ are reproduced by spores, and others by zoospores. The former method is analogous to that which obtains amongst ferns, while zoospores are cells that separate from the parent plant. In general, when reproduction is by spores, there are organs which in some senses correspond to the anthers and pistils of flowers. In the spore cavity or conceptacle, are certain bodies called *antheridia*, which fertilize the spores proper. Many of the green seaweeds are reproduced by *zoospores*, which method has been thus described by Dr. Harvey, the well-known phycologist : " In an early stage the green matter, or *endochrome*, contained within the cells of these algæ is of a nearly homogeneous consistence throughout, and nearly fluid ; but at an advanced period it becomes more and more granulated. The granules, when formed in the cells, at first adhere to the inner surface of the membranous wall, but soon detach themselves, and float freely in the cell. At first they are of irregular shapes, but they gradually become spheroidal. They then congregate into a dense mass in the centre of the cell, and a movement, aptly compared to that of the swarming of bees round their queen, begins to take place. One by one these active granules detach themselves from the swarm, and move about in the vacant space of the cell with great vivacity. Continually pushing against the sides of the cell-wall, they at length pierce it, and issue from their prison into the surrounding fluid, when their seemingly spontaneous movements are continued for some time. The vivacious granules, or zoospores, at length become fixed to some submerged object, where they soon begin to develop cells, and at length grow into algæ similar to those from whose cells they issued."

Not much need be said as to the apparatus for collecting and mounting seaweeds. An old knife and a few bottles for the more delicate species, with some sort of vasculum or satchel for the larger kinds, are all that will be required. The collector must not be above going bare-footed into the water now and then, unless he is provided with a pair of strong knee-boots ; for beyond where the lowest tide leaves its line of sea-wrack may be found many rare and choice specimens. At the same time, the drift that lies over all those parts of the shore that have been covered by the tide will well repay scrutiny.

As soon as convenient the specimens should be well washed in fresh water ; floated on to paper with careful fingers, helped, in the case of delicate kinds, by a quill pen or small camel's hair brush. The plan I find to answer best is to lay a sheet of thickish paper at the bottom of a large meat dish, and, after filling the dish with water, to place the specimen over the paper, and tease it out into as graceful a form as time and patience will permit.

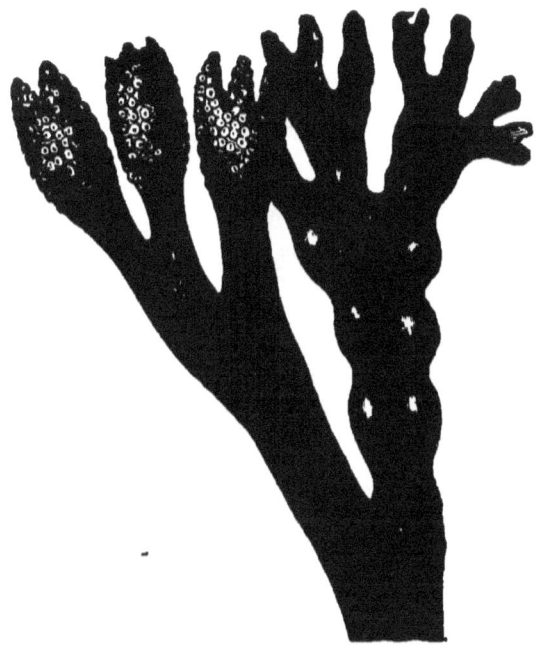

Fig. 2.—*Fucus vesiculosus.*

After this the mounts must be pressed and dried. When drained, spread over each a few strips of clean linen rags, which should be changed occasionally, care being taken to avoid disarranging the plants, and keeping them for a day or two under pressure. Many seaweeds are gelatinous, and will adhere to the paper without any medium. The large, coarse, olive-coloured weeds are not easily mounted for the herbarium, but small portions of them may be fastened on paper like dried plants,

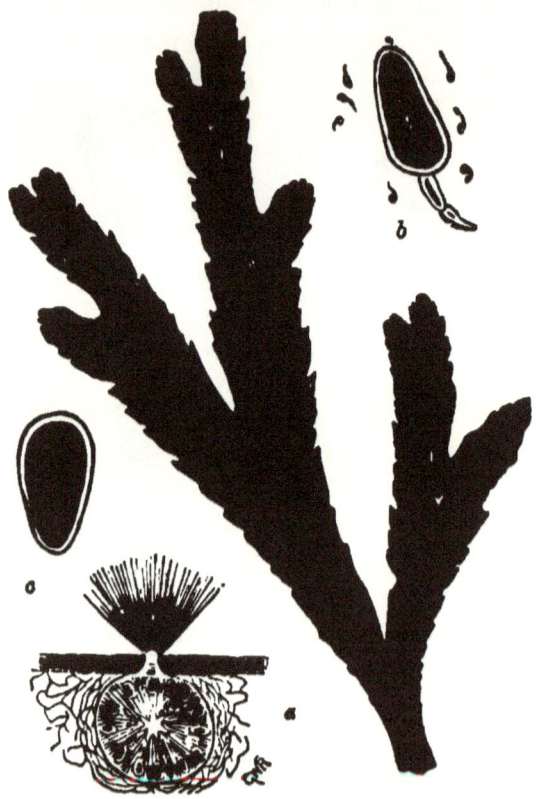

FIG. 3.—*Fucus serratus*, with conceptacle, spore and sporules.

while larger specimens merely require drying, and can be hung up for future reference, it being possible to restore to them much of their natural appearance by immersing them in warm water. For the identification of specimens a cheap and portable book is the one by Shirley Hibberd, published by Groombridge, which, for all ordinary purposes, is more serviceable than many a far costlier work. Landsborough's book is also cheap and useful. For more advanced work it will be necessary to procure some such treatise as Greville's or Harvey's on British Algæ.

The classification of seaweeds is a much simpler matter than is the case with more highly organized plants. It is curious that there is a direct relation between the colour and the mode of reproduction, so that, roughly speaking, the arrangement of seaweeds according to colour will correspond to botanical classification. The identification of genera and species, however, will require the microscope. There are three great primary divisions of marine algæ, viz. :—

(1) Olive-coloured (*Melanospermeæ*) ;
(2) Red (*Rhodospermeæ*) ;
(3) Green (*Chlorospermeæ*).

The olive-coloured kinds are mostly tough and strong ; many are furnished with air-vessels, and, in general, they grow near the shore. The commonest of these are the well-known Fuci (Greek *phycos*, a sea-weed), popularly called seawrack. The commonest of all is the Bladder-wrack, so called from the bladder-like air-vessels which cover it and by which it is kept floating in the water. *Fucus nodosus* (Fig. 4) is covered with large air-cavities. *F. serratus* (Fig. 3) has saw-like edges to the fronds, and is destitute of air-vessels. Another familiar species is the channelled Fucus (Fig. 1). These with several others were once largely used in the manufacture of kelp on account of their alkaline

FIG. 4.—*Fucus nodosus.*

constituents. *F. resiculosus* and *F. canaliculatus* are equally common at most English sea-side places (Figs. 1, 2). The celebrated Gulf-weed, *Sargassum bacciferum,* belongs to this order of *Fucaceæ.*

In the tide-pools near low-water mark occurs in many parts of our coasts the *Desmarestia,* whose fronds are flat and lance-shaped and pinnate, having spiny teeth on their edges. This may be taken as typical of the *Sporochnaceæ* or second order of olive weeds.

The most attractive of all the seaweeds with air-bladders is the Sea-oak or Halidrys (Fig. 5). It is found very generally on rocks and stones in the sea at nearly low water mark. Usually the fronds are about half a foot in length, though it is not uncommon to find them as long as three or four feet.

It is very much branched, and the branches are ornamented with curiously shaped air-chambers, which look like the pods of vetches, or of the mustard plant. These pod-like structures are even marked with transverse depressions, just as if there

FIG. 5.—*Halidrys siliquosa.*

were actually seeds inside, and so the illusion is increased.

Several of these Fuci are very useful. The Scotch used to gather them for kelp-making, but that industry has been superseded. They are still used as manure and as food for cattle, being mixed with meal. In the Hebrides the ashes of the

Bladder-wrack are used for drying cheeses, thus obviating the use of salt. These ashes contain about half their weight in alkaline salt. Its bladders also yield iodine, used largely for medicinal purposes. *F. serratus* is largely used for packing lobsters, and the channelled Fucus is eaten by cattle in the north of Britain.

The third order is called *Laminariaceæ*. The frond is flat and without midrib, and there is a kind of stalk. These grow below tide mark, but they are plentifully cast up, and very large specimens are dragged about by visitors to the seaside. *Laminaria* or Tangle is a good specimen for the study of the sucker-like "roots" which many algæ possess.

L. fascia, or the Papery Tangle, has a very short thin stem, and widens out into a long broad frond; one of the large tangles is called the Oar-weed. The Sweet *Laminaria*, or Sea-belt, makes a good hygrometer when hung up and will foretell rain.

The *Dictyotaceæ* include the Sea-endive, the pretty *Padina pavonia*, called so from its resemblance to a peacock's tail, the Girdle-weed or *Zonaria*, and *Taonia* or Peacock-weed, *Dictyota* or Netted sea-weed, *Stilophora* or Nettle-bearer, *Punctaria* and others.

The other orders of olive weeds are *Chordariaceæ* and *Ectocarpaceæ*, which include several lovely feathery plants.

Rhodospermeæ or red seaweeds are the most beautiful of all. Red is the prevailing colour, but a few brown, purple, and orange-tinted species are

included. The many-tubed *Polysiphonia*, whose
fronds are made up of thread-like tubular cells, is
well worth microscopical examination. There are a
score of British species, and many more on other
shores. *Laurencia* is abundant near low-water
mark, and is of a deep red colour. The Coral weed,
Corallina, has jointed pinnate fronds, and should
be sought for in the deeper pools. Young and
healthy specimens a r e
dark purple, but as picked
u p t h e y a r e usually
white. This is a very
curious plant, and scarcely
looks like a plant, being
pointed, and clad with a
coating of carbonate of
lime. If a portion be
placed in acid, the mineral
will dissolve, and the real
plant structure be plainly
discerned. *Nitophyllum*,
or Shining Leaf, is a very
fine weed, especially *N.*
punctatum, and may easily be found.

Fig. 6.—*Plocamium coccineum.*

One of the commonest, and at the same time one
of the prettiest, of the red seaweeds is the one called
Plocamium (Fig. 6). Its popular name is the Braided-
hair weed; indeed, *plokamos* means braided hair. Its
colour is a delicate pinky red. On account of its
elegant form and beautiful colour, it is one of the
chief favourites of those who arrange seaweed
ornaments. Although it lives beyond the shore-

line, yet it is cast up in abundance everywhere
along our coasts. The *Griffithsias*, called after
Mrs. Griffiths, the celebrated algologist, are all of
them exceedingly pretty.

One of the loveliest of the rhodosperms is *Mau-
geria sanguinea*, more familiarly known by its
older name of *Delesseria sanguinea*. It is very
common in the deep rocky pools. The Peacock's
Tail, or *Padina pavonia*, is well known, and is
largely used for ornamental patterns.

Chondrus crispus, or Irish Moss, called, by the
Irish, Carrageen, belongs to this second division
of seaweeds. When seen growing in the quiet
pools it appears very beautiful, and is of a deep
brown or purple colour, but in shallower water is
yellowish. The tasteless gelatine derived from it
is largely used in cooking, and at one time it
was credited with curative properties in cases of
consumption. It is still used in making jellies,
and even for blanc-mange, by confectioners. One
of the species of chondrus constitutes the material
from which Chinese birds make those edible nests
which are so highly prized by Oriental epicures.
Griffithsia, which has already been referred to,
is a widely distributed and pretty genus. All the
species are of delicate texture, and must not be
kept too long in water, or they will lose their
colour. The palmated *Rhodymenia* or Dulse is eaten
in Ireland, and is also dried for use as tobacco.

The third division of marine algæ consists mainly
of green weeds.

The commonest of these, indeed one of the

commonest of all seaweeds, is *Codium tomentosum,*
the Woolly Skin-weed. It is of a fine dark green
colour, and may be found in the deep rock-pools
that are never left dry. Its texture is sponge-
like, and it is covered with delicate filaments. A
prominent order of this group is that which com-
prises the *Ulvaceæ.* The best known of these are
the black-green *Porphyra,* the *Enteromorpha,*
nearly as common as *Codium,* called so because
of its intestine-like tubular fronds, and the bright
green, flat, and delicate *Ulva,* whose membranaceous
frond, waved at the margin, grows sometimes to a
length of two feet.

With one or two exceptions specimens of all
the foregoing, besides many others not referred to,
lie before me, the results of a few days' exploration
of a mile or two of shore ; and as I glance over
these plant-pictures shining out from their white
background, they revive for a while the delight
with which I sought and gathered them, and something of the awe which the great solemn ocean
awakened in the mind while its lovely treasures
were being culled comes upon me even now while
I admire them. What produces devouter or more
enduring impressions than to walk along the margin
of the murmuring sea, stopping now and again to
examine the wonders it casts up at our feet ; or to
gaze over its expanse stretching out to where it
seems to touch the sky, as though to bring into
relief our littleness of knowledge, and at the same
time to suggest the vastness of our intellectual
capacities ?

" Nature hath tones of magic deep, and colours iris bright,
  And murmurs full of earnest truth, and visions of delight ;
  'Tis said, ' The heart that trusts in her was never yet
    beguiled,'
  But meek and lowly thou must be, and docile as a child.
  Then study her with reverence high, and she will give the
    key,
  So shalt thou learn to comprehend the secrets of the sea."

There are many marine algæ besides these larger
ones, which never fail to give delight to those who
will take the trouble to look for them, minute and
indeed invisible, and requiring the microscope for

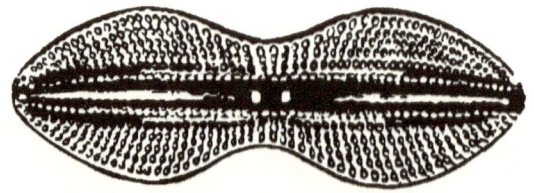

FIG. 7.—*Navicula didyma.*

their detection.   They are common enough, but
they are passed over unconsciously by all but the
thorough student of the wonders of the shore.
These are the Diatoms, whose glassy coverings or
valves are familiar to every one who possesses a
microscope (Figs. 7, 8). It is scarcely possible to avoid
collecting diatoms if anything at all wet is gathered.
Weeds, muddy or sandy sediment from tidal pools,
damp caves, stones, in fact everywhere, these
interesting organisms are met with.   If obtained
in a living state, their curious locomotion, which
led the older naturalists to class them amongst
animalculæ, may be studied ; and if dead, their

beautiful frustules provide valuable material for mounting for the microscope. Their movements seem to be wholly mechanical, and there is no trace of any self-directive power. They are of a jerky nature, and are quite aimless and uncertain.

So prolific are these tiny plants that their accumulated valves make large deposits in some places, as is the case at Dolgelly, Mull, and elsewhere in Britain. The entire city of Richmond, in Virginia, is built upon a bed of these diatoms eighteen feet in thickness. In Bohemia there is a deposit of them fourteen feet thick, from which is obtained that fine material used for delicate castings. I have a tin of diatomaceous earth from Hanover, known as Kieselguhr, or flint mud, which consists of very little else than the frustules of diatoms. This is the material which is used in the manufacture of dynamite, since it has the property of absorbing three times its weight of nitro-glycerine, thus presenting a remarkable illustration of combined feebleness and power. Tripoli powder and rotten stone, used for polishing, are similarly constituted. It is no exaggeration to say that, notwithstanding their extreme minuteness, these organisms have added more to the fossiliferous contents of the earth than all the great mammals put together.

The external covering or shell of diatoms is made up of two portions or valves, usually called frustules ; but there is no hinge connection, as in the case of molluscous bivalves. The two frustules are connected by a layer of silica, which runs round their

edges. This flinty covering is perforated, in order
to allow of communication with the outer world.

The minuteness of these plants is marvellous
when we bear in mind how perfect they are in every
detail of their form and markings. The giants
amongst them are not more than about one-fiftieth
of an inch·in length, while the majority are less
than one-thousandth of an inch. My friend, Mr.
Isaac Robinson, of Hertford, who has made these
organisms a special study, relates that one of his
slides which contains the frustules from a single
drop of water has upon it no less than 200,000
frustules, and another reaches the astonishing number of 430,000. And the water itself has to be
taken into account in attempting to form an idea of
the size of these infinitesimal inhabitants of that
small world. If the bulk of the drop of water had
consisted exclusively of frustules, there would have
been, in the latter case, upwards of ten millions.
How much truer it appears now than Shakespeare
ever imagined when he made Hamlet say, "There
are more things in heaven and earth, Horatio, than
are dreamt of in our philosophy !"

The utmost diversity of form is met with amongst
these minute plants. They are boat-shaped, triangular, square, crescent-like, filamentous, and seaweed shaped ; in fact, there is scarcely any conceivable pattern which does not find its counterpart
amongst these extraordinary objects.

The mounted frustules of Diatoms are extensively
used as tests for the determination of the quality
of microscopic lenses. An illustration of one of

these is given. It is called *Pleurosigma formosum*
(Fig. 8). For this object I must go to my cabinet
and take out one of the slides there stored, and
which has been properly prepared by a professional
mounter.

The silicious valves of Diatoms are beautifully
marked with ridges, called costæ, connected with an
inner membrane ; besides which there are numerous
dots, more or less minute, along the outside membrane. Generally the dots are arranged in regular
lines or series, radiating from the median line or
costa. . With a low power these rows of dots look

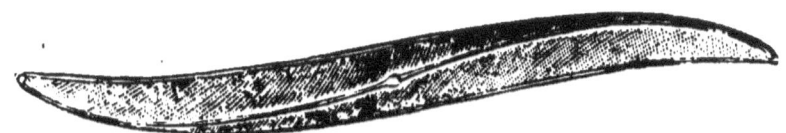

FIG. 8.—*Pleurosigma formosum.*

like continuous lines or striæ. Supposing that the
diatom has been properly cleaned and well mounted,
the striæ can be resolved into dots by objectives of
the requisite quality and magnifying power. As
the fineness of the dots varies in different species
(it is the character of these markings that determines
the species), it must not, of course, be expected that
a lens which will show the dots on one will necessarily do so on another. Certain well understood
species, therefore, are usually adopted by the
microscopist for testing lenses, and some of these
are commonly referred to as to a sort of standard by
which they describe the capabilities of an objective.
The costa is always visible, then the lines or striæ

3

are brought into view ; and lastly, if the lens is
equal to the proper test, the dots start out into dis-
tinctness. It may be as well, however, to remark
that the practised microscopist can often bring out
dots by manipulating his light and condensers
where the tyro would altogether fail. Some frustules do not exhibit the dot structure, but appear
to be ornamented with ridges. But however highly
magnified, the dots where they are shown are
all geometrically perfect, and not one of the
many thousands is ever found out of its proper
place.

Pleurosigma formosum has been chosen as one of
the most useful of these tests, and the appearances
which it presents under the quarter inch, one-eighth
inch, and one-twelfth inch objectives, may soon
become familiar to the student. Another species,
P. angulatum, is a good test for still higher powers ;
while none but the very best lenses will resolve into
dots the markings on *Amphipleura pellucida*, one
of the fresh-water species. There are, of course, many
other test objects besides diatoms, but these furnish
a very easy and reliable means of examining lenses,
and they have the great advantage of permanency
in regard to shape and appearance, a vital feature
of a reliable standard.

To mount the valves of Diatoms so as to preserve
them they should be put into a solution of sulphuric
acid. When the effervescence ceases it is an indication that all organic matter is destroyed. They
must then be washed and treated with nitric acid,
and washed again till nothing but dust is left. This

dust will be found crowded with the most bewitching forms, and is well worth mounting for future entertainment and study.

Diatoms are propagated usually by cell-division. By this process one cell becomes two, and these again divide. The cell-contents first divide, and each portion begins at once to grow a new valve. When this is completed the two parts separate, each possessing one of the old valves and a new one, and thus two perfect plants replace one old one. Professor Smith studied these processes some thirty years ago, and came to the conclusion that self-division occupied about twenty-four hours. If this is correct, the progeny of a single diatom would amount to a thousand millions in a month. This process is analogous to gemmation, and is something like the growth of a tree by budding. After awhile, however, the vital energy of the cells seems to be exhausted, and then a true generative process is set up. The cell contents of two parent frustules unite in some mysterious way and produce new generations.

Of these microscopic Algæ the number of species is simply bewildering. It is so recently as 1824 that Agardh published the first systematic arrangement of them, and he recorded forty-nine species. Now, however, they are numbered by thousands. Their exhaustive study is quite enough to occupy the whole leisure of any one individual, and it is not to be expected, therefore, that I can give here a complete account of them. But let it not be thought that they are contemptible or unworthy of investigation on account of their diminutive dimensions. There are very few objects in Nature which afford such pleasure to those who carefully examine them, and, moreover, it is by studying these minuter forms of life that we obtain light on the most profound problems of existence.

II.

" We turned, we wound
About the cliffs, the copses, out and in,
Hammering and clinking, chattering stony names
Of shale and hornblende, rag, and trap, and tuff,
Amygdaloid and trachyte, till the sun
Grew broader towards his death, and fell, and all
The rosy heights came out above the lawns."

TENNYSON.

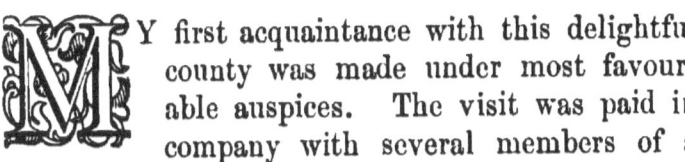Y first acquaintance with this delightful
county was made under most favour-
able auspices. The visit was paid in
company with several members of a
scientific society to which I belong, and the main purposes of it were geological. The field is one that has
attracted the attention of many leading geologists ;
and no knight of the hammer can fail to respond
to its fascination when once he finds himself in the
midst of its enchanting scenery. Peach, Pengelly,
Phillips, Le Neve Foster, Sedgwick, De la Bêche,
Bonney, all these have studied the Cornish rocks,
and given us the results of their observations.
There are in Cornwall several influential scientific
societies, such as the Geological Society of Cornwall

and the Mining Institute, and it was by the help
of these that our way had been so prepared as that
we found it easy to obtain access to everything
that a geologist might wish to see.

Operations were commenced at Truro, where we
were conducted over the new cathedral, just then
on the eve of being opened. After this the valuable
museum of the Royal Institution of Cornwall was
inspected, and then we threw ourselves in earnest
into the organized plans for the day, namely, to
visit several works connected with one of the most
remarkable developments of modern industry in
Cornwall—the quarrying and preparation of China
Clay.

Do not let any of my readers imagine that China
clay is at all like London clay,—either the slippery
material that one walks upon at Sheerness when
the tide is out, which the geologists call London
clay; or that abomination of the metropolitan
streets too familiar to many who are not geologists.
It has no affinity whatever with these, nor any
likeness to them. Emblematical of Cornish character, it is almost spotlessly white.

First, I must say a word or two about the name
of this interesting commodity. It is called China
clay, because it was in China that it first became
known. For many ages the Celestials manufactured
their beautiful ware without a rival. So successful
were they in guarding the secret of its composition
that it was only within quite recent times that a
Jesuit missionary was able to send a sample of
the crude material to Europe. The Rev. Hilderic

Friend, who has resided in China, recently sent me a note on this point, in which he observed that "a learned Jesuit missionary, P. Dentrecolles, tells us that the matter of chinaware is composed of two sorts of earth, one called Pe-tun-tse, and the other Kao-lin ; this latter is mixed with shining particles, the other is simply white and very fine to the touch." The Pe-tun-tse is the China stone and the Kao-lin is the China clay.

It is rather more than a century since China clay works were originated in Cornwall. About that time a Mr. W. Cookworthy, who had given considerable attention to porcelain-making, received some specimens of Kao-lin and of ware made therefrom. Not long afterwards he was fortunate enough to discover a large quantity of the substance in its natural state at St. Stephen's, in Cornwall. Very soon several works were established, and now that the secret was out the material was found abundantly in many other places. It seemed as if the declining industries connected with copper and tin had at length met with a successor which was to provide employment for some, at least, of those whose occupation was going. At the beginning of this century there were about half-a-dozen China clay works in operation, and nearly 2,000 tons were annually shipped from the county. Now, however, so rapid has been the development of the industry, nearly half-a-million tons are exported every year.

The next matter I ought to try to explain is the mode in which China stone and China clay occur in nature. One of the most convenient places for

studying this is at the works of the West of England
China Clay Company at Nanpean, near St. Austell.
It was here that the party of which I was a member
had the opportunity of observing all the processes
through which the natural product has to go, from
its extraction out of the earth to its final washing
and baking that fit it for the potter.

Every one knows that there are enormous quantities of granite in Cornwall. Granite used to be
regarded as the basic or foundation rock of the
earth's strata, but it is now known to have burst
its fiery way through various strata during almost
every geological period, and it was the upheavals
or eruptions of the molten masses which afterwards
cooled in the form of granite that transformed the
barren schists of Cornwall into rocks that are veined
with metalliferous lodes. Geologists are of opinion
that the series of extensive granite bosses which
stretch from Dartmoor to the Scilly Islands first
appeared after the deposition of the Upper Devonian
rocks. In fact, the leading feature of Cornish
geology now may be described as a group of granite
islands protruding out of a sea of Devonian schists.
The composition of granite, though varying in
different districts in regard to minor characteristics,
is mainly a mixture of quartz, mica, and felspar.
In some kinds the grains are very small, while in
others huge quartz crystals are seen an inch or
more in length. About half the bulk of granite is
made up of felspar, which is in reality hardened
volcanic lava. Cornish felspar is a silicate of
alumina and potash.

Now, it is this felspar in the granite that furnishes
us with China clay. It might seem an impossible
thing to a person with a lump of hard granite in
his hand to get the felspar out of it and to break
up that felspar into silica and potash at any such
cost as would make it worth while to do so. And
certainly it would be an utter impossibility for man
to do this at anything like a remunerative outlay.
But Nature does the work without effort and without
expense. By certain natural processes, the felspar
of the granite is decomposed, and the rock is transformed into a soft crumbling mass, which in many
places can be scooped out with the hand. The
potash and part of the silica are washed away, and
the silicate of alumina which remains constitutes
the China clay of commerce. China stone is this
same clay at a somewhat earlier stage in the process
of decomposition, when there is more of the quartz
mixed with it. Sometimes the clay comes nearly
up to the surface, but generally there is more or
less of sand and stones overlying it. This "over-
burden," as the covering is called, must, of course,
be removed before the clay is worked.

As may be supposed, geologists and chemists
have taxed their ingenuity in order to account for
this remarkable dissolution of the granite and felspar.
Carbonic acid, one of the strongest solvents in nature,
was, of course, invoked to explain the phenomenon.
But why has not this agent led to the disintegration
of granite in other places? Besides, could carbonic
acid act at such vast depths as those at which it is
known the clay occurs? Mephitic vapours are also

had recourse to, and these, no doubt, accompanied
the intrusion of the granite and the metals into the
rocks through which they poured when in a state
of fusion. Mr. J. H. Collins, who has paid great
attention to this subject, is of opinion that the
decomposition of the felspar and the consequent
formation of the Kaolin arose from the long continued action of water or steam containing hydro-
fluoric acid.   Traces of fluor are met with in the
granite at many places, and frequently the Kaolin
is in proximity with metalliferous veins, while in
many cases the clay deposits run along for miles in
the direction of tin veins, although they may be
only a few feet in breadth.

The outside surface-workings are very interesting.
Generally the clay has to be raised from a lower
level than the neighbouring ground. To effect this
a shaft is sunk, and from the bottom of this a level
is cut out underneath the clay that is to be worked.
An artificial arrangement of water channels leads
to the wearing down of the clay, which then hangs
suspended in the water, and this is pumped up from
the pit to the surface, usually to a somewhat higher
level than the ground, so as to allow of subsequent
operations and washings to be carried on by the
down-flowing of the water under the action of
gravity. In the wider channel the sand is deposited ; in the next, the finer mica is obtained,
which is not quite without value. The stream,
thus gradually purified, passes on to the first pits,
in which the clay settles to the bottom, and the
water runs off to be used over and over again. In

these pits the mixed water and clay look quite milky, and it is not at all unlikely that the tourist may suspect that he has discovered the source of Cornish cream—you must not say Devonshire cream in Cornwall or you are sure to be rebuked for your levity—but let us hope that cows are as plentiful in Cornwall as China clay is abundant.

The clay is taken from the "pits" into the tanks, where the fluid gradually becomes thicker, and after that it is poured into long, shallow pans built over flues. Here the drying process goes on until the substance is firm enough to bear being cut into squares of about nine inches. After a time these squares may be shovelled out, and the blocks of clay are ready to be transported to the pottery. If Cornwall were only blessed with coal, it might rival the Severn and Staffordshire. But the making of porcelain requires such great heat that the cost of bringing coal to the clay renders Cornish potteries an impossibility. It is cheaper to send the clay to the coal than to bring the coal to the clay.

Besides being used in the manufacture of porcelain, China clay is of importance to calico makers and bleachers. It is unfortunate, however, that it does not remain in the "pores" of the calico, which it whitens and thickens, and hence the fabric does not retain its apparent excellence when it has been through the hands of the laundress. Large quantities are taken also by paper manufacturers, for the purpose of giving body and weight to their paper. Some other applications of the article, the character of which is not quite beyond suspicion, are resorted to ; and, on the whole, it must be confessed that China clay in its uses has not won a reputation that harmonises with its pure and spotless appearance.

It would not be easy for the holiday-maker to find a more delightful way of spending a bright summer day than to take this walk from St. Austell to Nanpean and back, or, if he prefers to drive, as we did, to include in the excursion the open works of Carclaze and Minear Downs. In these latter places he will see strings of tin ore and schorl or tourmaline in the decomposed granite ; and, indeed, there is scarcely a spot he will pass but will furnish food for admiration and enjoyment. And if he be devout as well as thoughtful, he will not fail to recognise the wisdom and goodness of Him who " setteth fast the mountains," and yet maketh them to yield up their treasures for man's use and happiness.

On our return to Truro, we were entertained at the rooms of the Royal Institution of Cornwall, where the President and several members of the Council were assembled to give us welcome, and where we had a good opportunity of examining a capital selection of Cornish rocks and minerals.

The tin industries were the next objects of attention. The first excursion for this purpose was to Carn Brea, where the granite is seen in all its glory, and to the mining district of Redruth and Camborne. Cook's Kitchen, the oldest mine in the county now at work, Dolcoath, the deepest mine in the West of England, and others, were visited, under the guidance of Captain Josiah Thomas, who gave us most valuable and lucid information in regard to every point that called for remark. Speaking of Dolcoath mine, he said that the present workings were started in 1799. The mine was three-quarters of a mile long, a quarter of a mile wide, and over 400 fathoms deep from the surface. Out of that piece of ground there had already been obtained three and a half millions of pounds' worth of copper, and nearly the same of tin. The total outlay had been £40,000, and they were making about £50,000 a year profit. The mine shows no tendency to exhaustion, but, on the contrary, gets richer as the depth increases. I must not stay to describe all the various kinds of machinery by which the men go up and down the mines, and by which the ore is crushed and dressed, and prepared for the smelter ; nor must I attempt to tell how royally we feasted at the Tehidy mansion of the Bassetts, or how instructive were the speeches that were delivered after the luncheon. On subsequent days, Land's End and Cape Cornwall were visited, and other mines were examined, one of the most notable of which, Botallack mine, runs out under the sea ; but no special reference need be made to these.

Tin is obtained mainly from cassiterite, or tin-stone, so far as Cornwall is concerned ; but lodes rich enough to require little preparation for the smelter are very rare. After the tin-stone has been broken into lumps, it passes through the " stampers," which may be called huge hammers.

Here the lumps are reduced to a fine grain, which
undergoes various washings. When purified from
all foreign matter, so far as washing can effect this,
the tin is smelted. By the kindness of Messrs.
Bolitho, we were enabled to watch the entire process, which was fully explained to us by Mr. A. K.
Barnett, F.G.S., of the Penzance Smelting Works.
The crushed ore is first mixed with "culm," or
anthracite, and subjected to a heat that causes it
to glare like the sun and bubble like boiling water.
The white tin is then run off into pans, and is
refined by forcing green wood into the bath. The
ebullition which ensues produces a frothy dross that
has to be removed. Then the tin, still molten, is
poured into vessels of various sizes, in which it
remains till it becomes solid. When this final
stage of the operations was reached, we had the
satisfaction of each receiving a small medal of the
refined tin, stamped with Messrs. Bolitho's trade
mark, a pleasing memento of our visit.

Tin-mining in Cornwall has seriously suffered
from the rich deposits that are now being worked
in Australia and America. During the last ten
years, more than a hundred mines have ceased to
work. Copper, too, though never of anything like
equal importance with tin in Cornwall, has gone
on gradually decreasing in the quantity obtained.

Next to the granite and metalliferous deposits,
the most interesting Cornish rock is the Serpentine,
a tough, compact stone, which is often veined so
beautifully as to make it valuable for decorative
purposes. It forms a large portion of the Lizard

district, where it may be seen in the high cliffs, intruding into the slates, and sometimes itself invaded by another igneous rock called Gabbro. It is curious that this Serpentine, forming a kind of plateau in a basin of surrounding hornblendic schists, may be identified by means of the pretty Cornish heath, *Erica vagans*, which grows on the Serpentine in great profusion, and scarcely anywhere else. De la Bêche supposed that the Serpentine appeared during the deposition of the Killas or Devonian clay-slates ; and it is clearly an eruptive rock like the granite. It is impossible to describe the delight we experienced in rambling over this peninsula, climbing the Logan Rock, which, though hundreds of tons in weight, could yet be made to swing by a mere push ; gazing at the white and golden sands of Kynance Cove, and exploring the wondrous caves which the devouring sea has eaten out of the hard cliffs in many a place.

Igneous and metalliferous rocks are so general and so important in Cornwall that no apology need be offered for this somewhat lengthy, yet all too scanty, description of them ; for, indeed, very little else remains to be remarked in the geology of this county, the stratified rocks being rarely met with.

CAMBRIAN.—Mr. Collins has described the old slates which are seen near Camborne, Ponsanooth, etc., as Cambrian ; but no fossils have been found in them.

SILURIAN.—In the Fowey beds, ichthyolites are found, while at Gorran Haven several species of brachiopods and trilobites enable the age of the beds to be discovered.

DEVONIAN.—The beds of this age consist of the well-known Killas, and through them vast bosses of granite have burst their way. On St. Michael's Mount, the junction of the granite and the Killas was distinctly traced out for us by Sir W. W. Smyth, who, in this excursion, conducted our party, and entertained us at his summer villa close by.

CARBONIFEROUS.—These are the Cornish "culm-measures," and are situated on the north coast, too far out of our line of march to be visited.

Until recently, no formation has been known in Cornwall newer than the Palæozoic, unless some of the "elvans" or dykes of quartz-porphyry running out from the granite be newer, as they certainly are more recent than the granite which has burst through the Devonian Killas. But, within the last few years, a most interesting bed has been discovered near St. Erth. While digging for clay for the Penzance dock, a number of marine shells were met with. These turned out to be identical with the fossils of the Pliocene or Red Crag, which every visitor to Walton-on-the-Naze has seen. Here a busy hour was spent by our company; and I was able to obtain a good supply of Nassa, Turritella, and a few other things. Can it be that this deposit means that the sea, so recently as the Pliocene age, stretched from the Atlantic away to the Mediterranean, where similar fossils are found, and that the deposits of the crag period have since been denuded from the entire tract of country

between Cornwall and Norfolk? This is a question
suggested by the opening up of this modern bed
in the bosom of Palæozoic Cornwall, and shows
the importance of the discovery.

Time fails me to tell of the innumerable other
interesting walks and drives which helped to fill up
that sunny week. What delightful clambering we
had over the crags of St. Michael's Mount, glittering
here and there with valuable streaks of mineral!
what glorious rides on brake and coach through the
winding lanes, whose tangled banks gave constant
interest to the botanist! How gleefully we scampered
over fields to pluck a root of chicory growing wild
in profusion, or through quiet glens filled with the
restful music of the babbling brook, where flourished
in all its glory the Queen of Ferns, *Osmunda
regalis!* With what indescribable emotions we paddled
about bays and coves in the deepening gloaming,
watching the bright phosphorescence which at
intervals flashed along the ripples of water made
by our oars and keels! These and many other
marvels must be passed over, but they can never be
forgotten. A tour like this, during which some of
the secrets and beauties of nature are beheld in the
company of those who know how to interpret them,
leaves influences and lessons of life-long import.
I cannot resist the temptation to quote a passage
from Quatrefages' charming pages, which more
than any words that I can conceive gives a description, so far as such feelings can be described, of the
sentiments which again and again filled my mind
during the fleeting hours spent on the gleaming

4

strands of those Cornish coves, or on the quiet
waters of those Cornish bays, or on the wild
rugged cliffs that rib them round as with impregnable barriers : "If you still preserve any of
those illusions which, day by day, are vanishing
amid the turmoils of life, if you regret the dreams
that have fled never to return, go to the ocean side,
and there on its sonorous banks you will assuredly
recall some of the golden fancies that shed their
radiance over the hours of your youth.   If your
heart have been struck by any of those poignant
griefs which darken a whole life, go to the borders
of the sea, seek out some lonely beach, beyond
reach of the exacting conventionalities of society, and
when your spirit is well-nigh broken with anguish,
seek some elevated rock, where your eye may at once
scan the heaving ocean and the firmament above ;
listen to the grand harmonious voices of the winds and
waves, as at one moment they seem to murmur gentle melodies, and at another swell in the thundering
crash of their majesty ; mark the capricious undulations of the waves, as far as the bounds of the
horizon, where they merge into the fantastic figures
of the clouds and seem to rise before your eyes into
the liquid sky above.   Give yourself up to the sense
of infinitude which is stealing over your mind, and
soon the tears you shed will have lost their bitter-
ness ; you will feel ere long that there is nothing
in this world which can so thoroughly alleviate the
sorrows of the heart as the contemplation of nature,
and of the sublime spectacle of creation, which leads
us back to God " (*Rambles of a Naturalist*, I. 120).

III.

"It is a lonely place, and at the side
Rises a mountain rock with rugged pride,
And in that rock are shapes of shells, and forms
Of creatures in old worlds."

CRABBE.

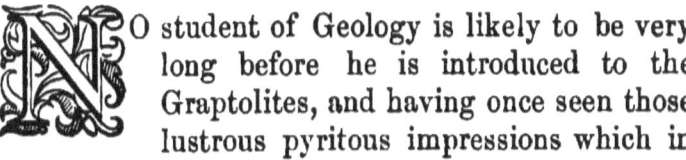O student of Geology is likely to be very long before he is introduced to the Graptolites, and having once seen those lustrous pyritous impressions which in many localities cover the Silurian slates as though with silvery hieroglyphics, he will never forget them. They are as curious as they are beautiful, and no extinct forms have given rise to more discussion respecting their structure and palæontological significance.

The name of these fossils was given to them from their resemblance to lines of writing, their similarity to some of the old inscribed stone slabs being very striking in the case of a not overcrowded layer of slate. They have never been found outside the Cambrian and Silurian systems, being most abundant at the base of the Silurian formation, and

in the upper Cambrian strata.   It will be seen then
that graptolites furnish a most valuable test of the
age of the rocks in which they occur.   For want
of a little information of this kind a speculator
some years ago spent a large sum in searching
for coal amongst the black shales of Tullygirvan

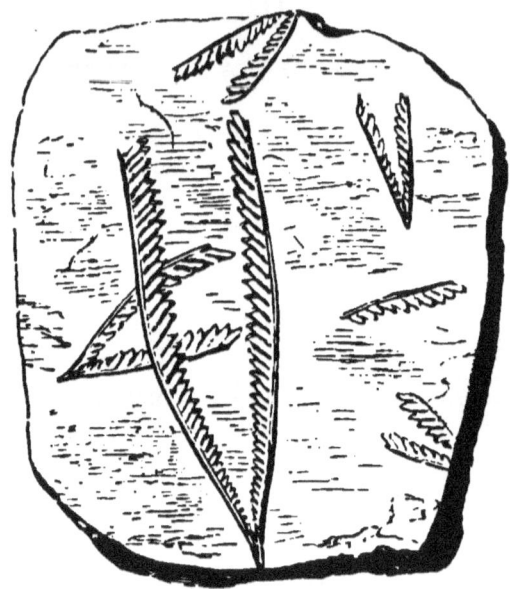

Fig. 9.—*Didymograptus Murchisoni.*

in Ireland, notwithstanding that every blow of the
pick revealed quantities of graptolites which would
have informed the merest tyro in geology that he
was working rocks that had been deposited vast
ages before the coal forests began to grow.

The best places in this country for obtaining
these most interesting fossils are the Lower Silurian
beds of Dumfriesshire, the soft shales of which are

easy to work, at Low-wood on the eastern side of Lake Windermere, in the slaty shales of the railway cutting near Conway station, in the slate quarries of Llansantfroid in Denbighshire, in the Arenig rocks of Port Madoc in North Wales, and of Ramsey Island, at St. David's, and other places in South Wales, in the Ludlow series of the Upper Silurians, and in the Wenlock shales of Builth.

The zoological characters of the graptolite are not easy to discover from their fossil remains, especially as there is no known living form with which they can be grouped. The truth is that our modern classifications, whilst extensive enough to include within their limits every organic form both extinct and surviving, require a few spaces to be left in which to place some fossilized remains of creatures that are totally unlike anything now existing. Graptolites are of this kind. While presenting a few similarities to the broader characteristics of Hydrozoa, they yet differ so radically from all other Hydrozoa as to lead Professor Nicholson to set them apart in a sub-class which he calls Graptolitoidea, corresponding to Allman's Rhab-

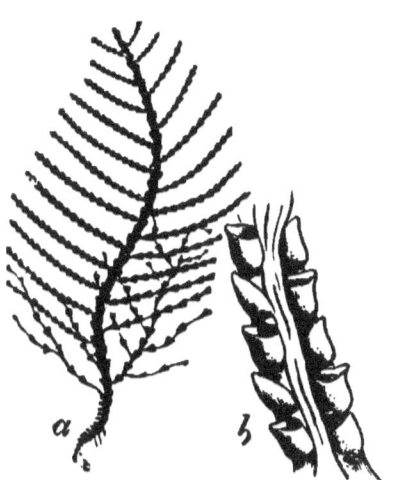

FIG. 10.—*Sertularia fusca*,
(*a*) Colony, natural size,
(*b*) Calycles, magnified.

dophora. Other allied groups of Hydrozoa are the
sub-class Hydroida, of which Hydra and Scrtularia
are known to every microscopist. The less known
sub-classes Siphonophora and Lucernarida, along
with the Hydrocorallinæ or Millepores, leading
on to Corals, the latter, however, belonging to
Actinozoa, which with Hydrozoa make up the
sub-kingdom of Cœlenterata.

Although Graptolites have very little in common
with any of these groups, yet it will be easier to
convey an idea of what their structure probably
was by drawing attention to the familiar Sertularia
or Sea-fir. A representation of one of these,
Sertularia fusca, is given (Fig. 10). The entire
colony, or polypary, as it is called, is seen at *a,* being
in appearance very much like a plant, and, indeed,
is picked up on the sea shore by multitudes who
suppose it to be a seaweed. At *b* is a magnified
view of a portion of the colony, where the shape
of the cups or calycles can be more easily made
out. These cups or cells are inhabited by polypes
or lowly jelly-like creatures. The stem is horny
and hollow, giving off many horny branches. The
polypes are connected with each other and with the
polypary by a fleshy tissue called the *cœnosarc*
(common flesh), which runs through the hollow
stems of the colony or hydrosoma. Occasionally
there will be found on the branches of the polypary
little capsules, called gonothecæ, which may be
seen by the naked eye, but must be magnified in
order to perceive their shape. These are concerned
in reproduction. The embryo emerges from these

as a free swimming animal, a sort of jelly fish, which, however, soon settles down and proceeds to establish a colony. Fig. 11 shows the magnified calycles, and also a much enlarged reproductive capsule of the common Sea-fir (*Sertularia abietina*).

For the purpose of comparison a portion of graptolite is added at Fig. 12, showing a magnified view of what are regarded as corresponding to the calycles or cells of Sertularia.

It is probable that Graptolites were in some respects similar to these Sea-firs. The

FIG. 11.—Sea-fir (*Sertularia abietina*) with magnified calycles and capsule.

double Graptolites (Fig. 13) look rather like Sea-pens (Pennatula). This led Page to regard them as allied to these members of the order of Actinozoa,

FIG. 12.—Calycles of *Didymograptus Murchisoni.*

but the resemblance is merely external. Others have ranged the Graptolites amongst Polyzoa, which gives them a still higher development, but there is very little justification for this. Few palæontologists or zoologists are more competent to decide such a question than Professor Nicholson of Aberdeen, who makes them a sub-class of Hydrozoa,

regarding them as nearly related to the Sea-firs
In support of this it is said that Mr. Hopkinson
discovered egg-bearing capsules (Gonothecæ) in
Graptolites. Nicholson figures what he calls
capsules in his monograph of the Graptolitidæ'

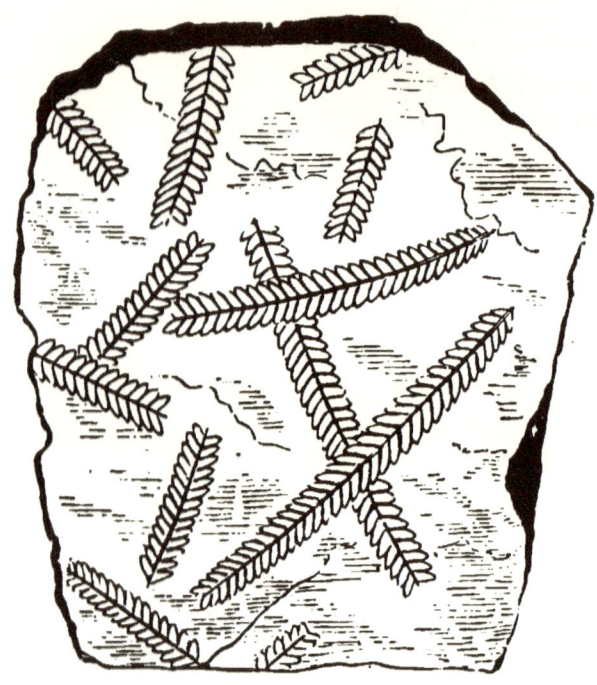

Fig. 13.—Double Graptolite (*Diplograptus pristis*).

which he found on some of his specimens. Fossil
Graptolites are of course destitute of all traces of
the animals which inhabited them, and we possess
very little more than the mere stems upon which
the polypes were seated. Professor Allman, however, doubts if these objects figured by Nicholson
really are egg-cases. He supposes that Graptolites

were not reproduced after the manner of Sertularians, but were developed by budding. The cups he thinks were filled with protoplasmic matter called *Nematophores.* From these characters he is induced to place the Graptolites as low down as Rhizopods. We are compelled, therefore, to leave the point in some degree of uncertainty, and to take the tolerably safe position of regarding these curious organisms as being nearly related to Sea-firs, while at the same time they possess some characters of the much lower class of Rhizopoda of which Foraminifera are familiar members.

These preliminary observations will, it is hoped, enable every reader to understand the following somewhat technical definition of Graptolitoidea given in Nicholson's *Manual of Zoology*, page 167: "Hydrosoma (the entire organism) compound, occasionally branched, consisting of numerous polypites united by a cœnosarc; the latter being enclosed in a strong, tubular, chitinous polypary, whilst the former were protected by hydrothecæ (cups). In the great majority of Graptolites the hydrosoma was certainly unattached; but in some aberrant forms—doubtfully belonging to the sub-class—there is reason to believe that the hydrosoma was fixed. In many cases the hydrosoma was strengthened by a chitinous rod, the solid axis or virgula, somewhat analogous to the chitinous rod which strengthens the polyzoary in the singular Polyzoon, Rhabdopleura. This axial rod lies in a groove on the dorsal side of the polypary (*i.e.* on the side opposite to that on which the hydrothecæ are developed), and it may be prolonged beyond one or both ends of the colony. The polypary is typically furnished at its proximal end with a minute triangular or dagger-shaped spine (sicula), which represents the embryonic skeleton."

Graptolites differ from Sertularia in possessing the axis and sicula, while it is quite certain that the typical forms were free swimming and not fixed as Sea-firs always are.

There are two main groups of Graptolites, one of which (monoprionidian) is characterized by a row of hydrothecæ or cups on one side only of the rod, whilst the other (diprionidian) has a row of cups on each side of the axis. There are others which have four rows of hydrothecæ (*Tetragraptus*). The diprionidian Graptolites are found in the Cambrian and Silurian rocks, the ordinary form (monoprionidian) being found only in the Cambrian. These two forms are illustrated by the ordinary twin Graptolite (*Didymograptus Murchisoni*) at Fig. 9 and the double Graptolite (*Diplograptus pristis*) at Fig. 13.

This discussion respecting the nature and affinities of Graptolites has a very important bearing on the evolution theory. It is significant that while marking so definitely a distinct geological period these interesting fossils appear and disappear with startling abruptness without any apparent cause, revealing such slender relationship to other animal groups as to make it quite impossible to rank them with any other organisms. The believer in the doctrine of special creation may certainly find much

to corroborate his views in the history of Graptolites,
especially if he be willing to take the moderate
position preferred by many Christian students of
science, namely, that creation was by method or
process—Divine law or even law of Nature it may
be called—operating sometimes slowly, as we see
it, and at other times rapidly, as though by special
manifestations of creative energy. In those remote
ages in which Graptolites flourished, types of life
seem to have swept in one after the other in waves,
as if some Supreme Power were forcing them on.
The leading groups of Palæozoic animals, Molluscs,
Crustaceans, Fishes, Reptiles, seem to have had no
ancestors, and can only be linked on to each other
by creations of the human imagination and by
supposing such vast geological blanks as we have
no right to take for granted. These views are
amplified by Professor Dawson in his *Chain of
Life*, from which the following quotation may fitly
be taken as the conclusion of this chapter : " The
progress of life is not gradual but intermittent, and
consists in the sudden and rapid influx of new forms
destined to increase and multiply in the place of
those which are becoming effete and ready to vanish
away or to sink to a lower place. Further, since
the great waves of aquatic life roll in with each
great subsidence of the land, a fact which coincides
with their appearance in the limestones of the
successive periods, it follows that it is not a struggle
for existence, but expansion under favourable circumstances, the opening up of new fields of
migration that is favourable to the introduction

of new species. The testimony of palæontology on
this point, in my judgment, altogether subverts the
prevalent theory of 'survival of the fittest,' and
shows that the struggle for existence, so far from
being a cause of development and improvement,
has led only to decay and extinction, whereas the
advent of new and favourable conditions, and the
removal of severe competition, are the circumstances
favourable to the introduction of new and advanced
species."

Opinions so authoritative, based upon such weighty
considerations, are deserving of respectful and careful attention, and should certainly make all who
desire to know the truth and to see it prevail receive
with the utmost caution any partial hypothesis which
requires so much aid from the imagination to make
it fit in to the demands of the case as do many of
the current theories and speculations concerning the
origin and development of life on the earth.

IV.

A VISIT TO THE CHANNEL TUNNEL.

" Life's needful functions, food, exertion, rest,
  By nice economy of Providence,
  Were ever ruled to carry on the work
  Which out of water brought forth solid rock."

MONTGOMERY.

NE of the most lovely and enjoyable walks that can be found on the Kentish coast is the one from Folkestone to Dover. The lofty chalk cliffs broken into infinite shapes by the action of the waves, the glittering pebbly beach making ceaseless music as the water ripples over it, the sparkling brightness of the sea as it gently rolls at the feet, all combine to make a picture of indescribable beauty. Some would prefer to wander along the upper cliffs, from which on a sunny day the coast of France is distinctly visible over the expanse of undulating billows, and to descend occasionally into the sheltered nooks formed by landslips of greater or less extent, where mare's tails grow profusely, and where now and then the blindworm, so like a young adder to the uninitiated, glides forth ; but he who has a geologist's tastes and a geologist's legs will soon haste down the broken slopes of the Folkestone Warren, and tramp the flinty shingle with unwearying feet, that he may feast his eyes on the magnificent sections of the chalk formations which are presented all the way along. If the tide is going out the walk under the cliffs is perfectly safe, and for a considerable distance the foreshore will prove a most attractive field to the hunter of fossils. Here is found one of the most accessible sections of the Gault, a dark stiff bluish clay, which lies at the very base of the upper Cretaceous strata, and described as being from 100 to 200 feet in thickness. Immense quantities of iron pyrites and phosphatic nodules lie about, some of them so smooth and spherical that paterfamilias may carry them home for marbles, while others are bright with sulphur, and present, when split open, the most graceful crystalline forms. But more valuable than these to the geologist are the swarms of Ammonites, many of them resplendent with the hues of mother-of-pearl, the numerous Belemnites, so called from their resemblance to a horny dart, the regularly grooved shells of the Inoceramus, the finely streaked Nucula, the curious Hamite, and many others, which are thickly strewn about. In some places the bed looks like one mass of fossils, and all around

> " Are shapes of shells, and forms
> Of creatures in old worlds, and nameless worms,
> Whole generations which lived and died ere man,
> A worm of other class, to crawl began."

During several visits, none of them of more than

a few hours' duration, I have collected the following :
Ammonites margaritatus, A. tuberculatus, A. inter-
ruptus, several other species of Ammonites, Belemnites minimus and others, Hamites rotundus,
Inoceramus sulcatus, I. concentricus, Rostellaria
carinata, Solarium, Nucula ovata, N. pectinata,
Natica Gaultina, Pleurotomaria Gibsii, Turrilites
elegans, Ostrea carinata, Pentacrinus Fittoni, Spine
of Echinus, Teredo, Carapace of Crab, Lobster, and
Saurian vertebræ. As there are some 250 species
at least recorded for the Gault it would be easy to
add to this list by remaining at Folkestone long
enough to take advantage of the most favourable
tides.

The hammer and chisel are of little use for the
Gault. Its fossil contents must be carefully cut out
with a knife, and even the most delicate handling
will not always secure them unbroken. Let the
amateur take up a ball of the plastic clay and
mould it with his hands into an apple-dumpling
shape, sticking upon it with as much artistic taste
as he possesses the various specimens picked up,
and this, when hardened by keeping, will make a
capital paper-weight for the study table, and will
serve as a miniature representation of the Gault.

But we must leave this fruitful necropolis of
ancient cretaceous beings, so fascinating to the
geologist, but a terror to the Channel Tunnel
engineers, and round the point which terminates
the Warren.

Now the chalk proper may be witnessed in all its
glory. From this spot to Lydden Spout the cliffs

rear themselves up almost perpendicularly from
high-water mark, and distinct bands of different
cretaceous deposits can be seen. At the bottom,
lying on the Gault, is a thin layer of chalk marl,
next above which is a thick band of grey chalk, the
delight of the tunnellist, and after this comes an
important deposit of white chalk without flints,
composed mainly of crumbled foraminifera and
mollusca, presenting under the microscope a remarkable similarity to the deep sea ooze of our own
time; while last of all is a layer of nodular chalk
containing many flints. It is said that these nodules
are simply petrified sponges, and that flints are of
similar origin. These animals—yes, sponges are
animals—long before we were born secreted great
quantities of silica from the water of the ancient
seas, which after the death of the sponges became
a nucleus around which were aggregated other
elements by chemical agencies, the whole hardening
afterwards into the unbreakable flints that are so
cordially hated by those who have the management
of the cutters in the Channel Tunnel operations.
But this is not the only theory afloat concerning
the origin of flints.

Near Lydden Spout some idea of the action of
the sea in wearing down rocks may be obtained.
A very useful path winding down from the coast-
guard station to the beach below has been quite
washed away for some distance at the bottom in
the space of a few months, and now the pedestrian,
if he should reach the spot when the water is coming
in, may find himself in serious difficulties. A little

farther along the South Eastern Railway Company are being compelled to pay attention to the foundations of their line. Enormous changes are attributed to this denuding power of the ocean, and it is supposed by most geologists that this " tight little island " has been gradually separated from the continent by the wear of ceaseless waves through years uncountable. It may have been, however, that more violent agencies had something to do with the existence of the "silver streak," and perhaps this rent in the earth's ribs was first started by some volcanic shock or spasm of earthquake. One advantage of being a geologist is that you have *carte blanche* to theorize, and you are not obliged to give yourself any trouble about proof. It is certain, however, that England was once joined to France, for there, on the other side of the twenty odd miles that separate perfidious Albion from her artless neighbour, are the clear evidences of the union which formerly existed. Layer after layer, from the Gault to the upper chalk, appears on the French coast, in exactly the same order and with perfect identity, as regards fossil contents and lithological structure, as are exhibited in the Folkestone and Dover cliffs. The dip, or inclination, of those strata is such as to demonstrate that the chalk bed which is most favourable for tunnelling operations lies almost horizontally across the Straits, and therefore, as Professor Boyd Dawkins, who led our party, drily remarked to us, "Providence evidently intended there should be a Channel Tunnel, whatever the Duke of Cambridge or Lord Wolseley may say."

5

The works of the " Submarine Continental Railway Co." lie under the shadow of the mighty
Shakespeare Cliff, which rises sheer up from the
beach to a height of 450 feet. At the first blush
the smoking chimneys·and grimy sheds strike the
spectator as a black and offensive spot on the fair
whiteness of the chalk background, but one has to
remind himself that this is a utilitarian age, and
has little patience with that sentiment which would
fain roll away the murky smoke from our leaden
skies, and hurl back the iron wheels that disturb
the solitude of every peaceful glen.

Admission into the works was obtained by a
written order bearing the signature of Sir E. W.
Watkin. Our *Open Sesame* had of course been
previously provided, and we were able to see all
that our eyes might have been trained to see.
Machines of various kinds, Swan's electric lighting
engines, powerful lifting machinery, and engines
for pumping air into the tunnel and water out of it,
all possessed a charm because of their association
with this great undertaking ; but of such things I
forbear to write, remembering the old proverb about
the cobbler and the last, which perhaps I ought
to quote rather in the dignified words of Apelles
when he rebuked an impertinent shoemaker who
dared to criticise a slipper in one of his pictures,
Ne sutor ultra crepidam.

The shaft, of course, is the chief object of interest
to the sight-seer. This descends to a depth of 160
feet, and constitutes the only outlet for the *débris*

of the tunnelling operations. If the tunnel should ever become *un fait accompli*, there will be inclined planes of considerable length on the two coasts, gradually leading to the bottom. It has, perhaps, not been generally understood through the country that the work has progressed so far as we found to be the case, and something like surprise was felt even by our legislators when the indefatigable " hecklers " of St. Stephen's elicited the fact that over two miles of tunnel had actually been completed. On the English side 2,400 yards, and on the French side 1,600 yards, have been excavated. At present the work is at a standstill, and seems likely to remain so if we may judge from the recent votes of Parliament.

Geologists and mining engineers are quite agreed as to the practicability of this gigantic undertaking. The problem of ventilation may be regarded as solved, and it is not likely that the atmosphere of the tunnel will ever be any worse than that of the Metropolitan Railway. The possibility of faults being encountered is a more formidable question, although it is not thought by experienced geologists that there can be any considerable alterations in the submarine strata. Professor Boyd Dawkins, who has measured and examined every foot of the rocks concerned, so far as they are accessible, is of opinion that the one care of the excavators must be to keep out of the Gault clay, and then such minor faults as might occur may be rendered harmless by the use of iron tubes, or by lining the exposed face with plates of iron cemented together. The French have already met with one of these fractures, but were able easily to get back into the right formation.

As regards the commercial advantages which this country would derive from the Channel Tunnel there is scarcely any division of opinion. The total exports and imports between England and the Continent reach an annual value of 400 millions sterling. Hence there must be considerable loss by damage, as well as delay, in loading and unloading, especially in cases of transhipment at London, all of which might be avoided if goods could be taken direct from this country to any part of Europe. The shipping interest has fiercely opposed the scheme ; and Mr. Henry Lee was even requested by a section of his constituents to resign his seat in Parliament on account of the evidence given by him before the Parliamentary Committee. The same spirit as that which Southampton manifested would have prevented the introduction of machinery into manufacturing industry, and so have checked the growth of England's prosperity and wealth. Mr. Giffen, of the Board of Trade, believes that ultimately the shipping interest would reap great benefit from the tunnel, for the loss now suffered is causing many to send their cargoes direct to the continental ports.

It has been urged as a reason for not carrying out the work that it might lead to a complete breaking down of all our healthy insular peculiarities,

and that in social and national life the English
would become assimilated to Continental ideas.
Some of our insular prejudices might with great
advantage be replaced by more cosmopolitan notions.
But why should not the reverse process take place
in the leavening of French society with English
sentiments and ideas ? Such objections, however,
are hardly worth considering, for they cut at the
root of all intercourse between nations, and would,
if carried to their logical issue, lead us into Chinese
exclusiveness and stagnation.

The weightiest objection against the construction
of the tunnel, and the one that is likely to prove
fatal to the scheme, is that which is raised by the
military authorities of the country. There would,
say our leading generals, be a standing danger in
the possibility of an enemy possessing himself of
the entire works, and so effecting an easy entrance
into our very midst ; and, moreover, in time of
diplomatic differences there would be the recurrence
of panics which might lead to the unnecessary
destruction of valuable property. Sir Lintorn
Simmons, Inspector of Fortifications, amused the
Committee of Inquiry by stating his opinion that a
government so insane as to permit a tunnel being
made, would be insane enough not to destroy it in
time of danger.

The idea of invading England by means of a
submarine passage is not a new one. There is an old
engraving in the *Bibliothèque Nationale* at Paris,
dated 1803, which shows that Napoleon, then First

Consul, had such a plan actually laid before him. The picture represents a tunnel crowded with soldiers and cannon, while the sea above swarms with vessels, and the air is filled with balloons.

It is admitted on all hands that the tunnel could be rendered useless in a few minutes, and war between civilised peoples never breaks out without considerable warning and preparation. Even France would not be capable of seizing the English defences and garrison by a *coup de main* without awakening previous suspicion.

The arrangements proposed for the temporary demolition of the tunnel are such as these : by means of a portcullis at the mouth of the tunnel, several lengths of rails could be immediately removed, and a trap-bridge raised. Ventilation could at once be stopped, and shingle in large quantities heaped up in the way of a hostile force. Besides which, it would be possible to carry alongside the tunnel, or underneath it, mine galleries in which dynamite could be permanently kept in sufficient quantities to render the tunnel impassable in a few seconds. Sluice-valves, also, might be so constructed as to flood the tunnel at a very short notice.

Of course, as Lord Wolseley has said, military arrangements are never in perfect order in time of peace ; but then it is not reasonable to suppose that all these arrangements, so simple and effective, would be found to be out of order at the same moment.

M. de Lesseps has lately said, "If the Channel Tunnel be not now completed, the glory of the work will belong to the next century, along with the right to wonder at our hesitations, and perhaps at our prejudices."

V.

DEAD SEA-LILIES.

" Here, too, were living flowers,
  Which, like a bud compacted,
  Their purple cups contracted ;
  And now in open blossom spread,
  Stretch'd, like green anthers, many a seeking head.
  And arborets of jointed stone were there."

SOUTHEY.

NY one looking at an encrinite for the first time would probably suspect that it was the remains of a dead flower. And when it was alive it was still more like a plant. But it is an animal, or rather a colony of animals. And though lying here in between the layers of a Silurian slab, or flattened out on a slice of Liassic shale, dead enough, and only the skeleton of its former self, it is sufficiently beautiful to justify us in calling it a dead Sea-lily.

Crinoids, the fossils of which are usually called Encrinites, belong to the sub-kingdom of Echinodermata, or spiny-skinned animals, which at one time Professor Huxley included with the lower worms (*Scolecida*) in the proposed sub-kingdom *Annuloida* or ring-like animals.

The star-fish and sea-urchin are the most familiar examples of echinoderms. Indeed, the sea-lily may be called a stalked star-fish. There are two types of Crinoids. (1) Sessile, which, after the developmental stages have been gone through, are not permanently fixed or " rooted," and hence are spoken of frequently as " free." A common living example of these is *Comatula rosacea.* (2) Stalked or pedunculated, which are permanently fixed when fully developed. *Apiocrinus rotundus* is a good example (*Frontispiece*). The column is often very long, and is composed of many joints, which are so articulated with each other as to give great flexibility to the stem.

A Crinoid may be described as an echinoderm having its body fixed, during a part or the whole of its existence, by means of a flexible stalk or column. The body is cup-shaped, and hence is called the " Calyx." It is covered with an external armour of calcareous plates, the upper surface being protected with smaller plates, loosely connected together by a leathery membrane. Its mouth is on the upper surface, thus differing from the star-fish, which has the mouth underneath. From the margin of the body spring five jointed arms, which sometimes subdivide, thus producing ten, or even fifteen, branches. These carry innumerable pinnules, and so form a cluster of delicate feathery plumes.

In regard to the mode of locomotion of larval and free Crinoids, the ambulacral, or water vascular system, respiration, and the nervous and reproductive organs, I must refer the reader to the text-books, only touching upon these points where it may be necessary to indicate any variations from the normal characters of living Crinoids that older forms may exhibit.

The earliest Encrinite is the *Dendrocrinus* of the Cambrian age.

In the Silurian deposits, particularly in the Wenlock limestone, vast numbers of encrinites have been obtained, and many of them of extreme beauty. The chief genera represented are *Glyptocrinus, Crotalocrinus, Marsupiocrinus, Cyathocrinus, Platycrinus, Taxocrinus, Icthyocrinus,* and *Edriocrinus.* We have selected as illustrations *Marsupiocrinus* (*marsupium,* pouch) and *Crotalocrinus,* so called from its similarity in shape to a child's rattle (Greek *krotalon,* rattle). The arms of *C. rugosus* begin at the top of the body, and the ossicles are fastened to each other both at the sides and vertically, thus giving the appearance of a basket-work rattle (Fig. 14).

The Devonian rocks also furnish large quantities of encrinites.

In the Carboniferous deposits encrinites are so numerous that it has even been suggested that the period to which they belong should be called "the age of Crinoids." From the Yoredales of Hebden Bridge very fine specimens have been obtained. It would seem as if the muddier sediments of the Yoredale deposits had proved suddenly fatal to vast quantities of these delicate organisms, just as we know would now be the case were the water in which the coral polypes are carrying on their mar-

vellous operations to become fouled with mud. No
one can have walked through the Peak District of
Derbyshire without having observed the "screw-
stones," or casts of encrinital stems which protrude

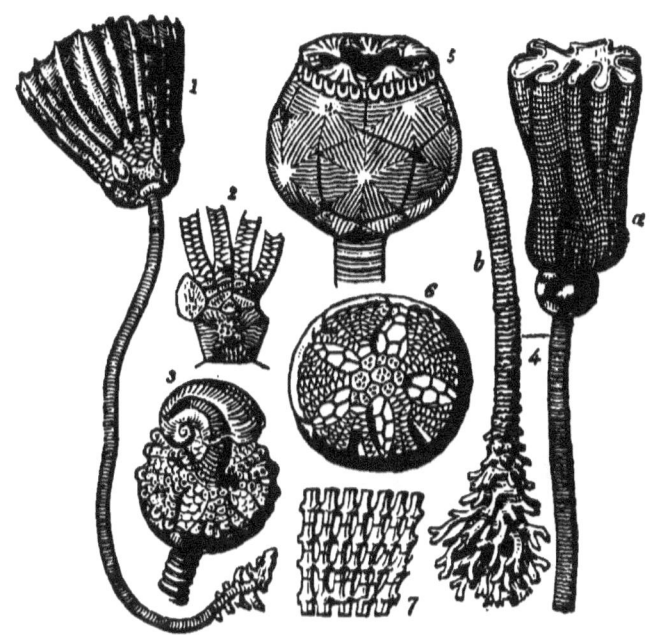

FIG. 14.—SILURIAN ENCRINITES—1. *Marsupiocrinus cœlatus.*
2. Base of arms, mag. 3. Proboscis, inserted in fossil shell.
4. *Crotalocrinus rugosus.* 5. Pelvis. 6. Flat stomach surface
and bases of arms. 7. Portion of 4a magnified.

from the limestone walls that form the boundaries
of the roads and fields all over that region. Most
of our readers also will be familiar with the lovely
black or mottled marble pieces variegated with
white markings of every conceivable shape, the
result of section through the fossil encrinites at

different angles. *Poteriocrinus crassus* (Fig. 15) is one of the most frequently occurring of the Derbyshire encrinites. The body or " head " is tapered in shape, thus resembling the little *Rhizocrinus Lofotensis* which has been dredged up alive from the depths of the North Sea by Dr. Carpenter and Sir Wyville Thompson. In other respects, however, *Rhizocrinus* finds affinities with an ancient race of

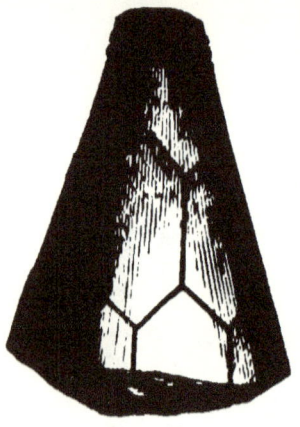

crinoids which flourished in Jurassic times, and of which *Apiocrinus rotundus* is a conspicuous specimen (*Frontispiece*). Other carboniferous crinoids are the genera *Actinocrinus, Cyathocrinus, Gilbertocrinus, Taxocrinus, Woodocrinus, Platycrinus.* Numerous as are the British Carboniferous encrinites, they occur in still vaster numbers in North America.

FIG. 15.

Head of *Poteriocrinus.*

Very few occur in the Permian strata. This does not mean that they had died out, for they reappear in large numbers in later epochs.

The Secondary encrinites are not so numerous as the Primary, but they are, in the main, of a higher type. The encrinites of the Secondary rocks mainly differ from those of the Primary in not having the grooves of the arms arched over, but the mouth and the grooves concerned in obtaining food were open to the surface and continuous, whereas the

Palæozoic crinoids mostly had the upper surface of
the calyx covered by a sort of dome, composed of
limy pieces of plates, the mouth and grooves not
being open to the surface. The grooves, in fact,
were veritable tunnels running to the mouth underneath the plates. These types are sometimes
referred to under the names Palæocrinoids and
Neocrinoids, but it would not be safe to regard these
terms, which were suggested by Dr. P. H. Carpenter,
as applying exclusively to geological age.

There are considerable numbers of encrinites in
the Triassic formations. One of the most beautiful
of all is the *Encrinus liliiformis,* which is peculiar
to the Muschelkalk of Germany, a deposit not found
in the English Trias. Its flower-like head is sup-
ported gracefully on a rounded stalk, the joints of
which are curiously articulated with one another,
while the fringed arms are each composed of a
double series of tiny plates of lime.

In the Jurassic deposits crinoids continue to be
common, more especially those belonging to the
genus *Pentacrinus,* the columns of which are five-
sided (pentagonal), having long slender arms.
Pentacrinus Briareus, so familiar to every visitor to
the Whitby Lias, possesses no less than a hundred
and fifty joints in the five pinnated arms of one
individual. These were covered with muscles and
an integument, which kept the innumerable ossicles
in their place, while the membrane was covered
with the minute cilia, the function of which was to
effect motion and propel the water down the grooves
that everywhere converged towards the mouth.

When found in the softer clays of Lincoln and
Whitby the joints are separate from each other,
and have for a long time been picked up and valued
as ornaments. In more ignorant and superstitious
days they were even supposed to have been the
relics of ancient personal decoration and the em-
blems of devotion. In Scott's *Marmion* we find
this myth referred to in the following lines :—

> " On a rock by Lindisfarne
> St. Cuthbert sits, and toils to frame
> The sea-born beads which bear his name."

Apiocrinus is a common Oolitic genus. The
crinoids of this group had a long column, which
was rounded and expanded at the uppermost joints,
forming with the summit a pear-shaped mass, and
hence obtaining the name of the Pear encrinite.
The organism was generally fixed to some hard
body, such as a shell, the base of the column being
spread out on the surface of such object just as the
common sea-weed (*Corallina officinalis*) arranges
itself on the sea-bed.

In the Jurassic rocks we meet with the more
highly developed crinoids, such as *Saccosoma*. This
greatly resembled the modern *Comatula*, or feather
star. When young it was attached, but like
Comatula it became free after having passed through
the larval stages. When the living larva of *Comatula* was first dredged up it was supposed to be
one of the fixed or pedunculated crinoids, and was
named *Pentacrinus Europæus*, but its true nature
is now well understood. It is generally held that

Crinoids are allied to the star-fishes through *Comatula* and *Euryale*, while they are linked on to the sea-urchins by the *Saccosoma* of the Oolites and the *Marsupites* of the Chalk.

A marked decrease in the number of encrinites is observable in the Cretaceous deposits. The stalked crinoids are represented by the genera *Pentacrinus* and *Bourgueticrinus*. Amongst the free crinoids are the feather-star and the tortoise en-crinites (*Marsupites*).

The process of diminution continued through post-Cretaceous times. In Eocene beds Crinoids are very poorly represented. But the forms which survive are for the most part those of highest development, such as the free or " sessile " *Comatula*, a typical example of modern living Crinoids.

VI.

A DAY IN A QUARRY.

"Go forth under the open sky, and list
To Nature's teachings."

BRYANT.

Y friend Baxter—though that is not his real name—happened to be spending his summer holiday in the vicinity of far-famed Malvern at the same time as myself. One bright morning, as I was just starting off for a geological ramble, he met me, and looking at me with a half-bewildered, half-amused stare at my leathern bag slung over my shoulder, and my thick walking-stick spud in my hand, he said, "Why, you surely have not turned rural postman, have you? Where in the world are you off to?"

"I'm going a-geologising," I replied; "you know the old saying, 'Blessed is the man who has a hobby.'"

"Well, you must be thrice blessed," he good-humouredly answered, "for you seem to have a number of hobbies. But what do you say to my going with you to-day? I've nothing particular on hand."

"Oh, I should be very glad of your company; but do you care to undertake a tramp of a dozen or fifteen miles this warm day?"

"I shouldn't think very much of that; you know I get some good walks on Sunday in our circuit."

"True," I answered; "you local preachers have the advantage of us ministers in that respect."

"And yet some of us think we should do a little better if we could get into the town pulpits rather oftener," said he, laughingly. "But I will just run in and tell them I am going with you."

"And, I say, just try to find a pair of boots with some soles on them, will you? A few sandwiches too would be useful. I have some business to do at the post-office, so I will meet you there."

Baxter soon joined me, and we started off on the road that led out of the town.

"Where are you making for?" he asked.

"What a question to ask a geologist!" said I; "it would be impossible for me to tell you, my dear fellow."

"Why, do geologists never know where they are going to? Perhaps that accounts for some of the curious conclusions they arrive at," said he, with a significant smile.

"Which remark is an allegory, I suppose," replied I. "You know a geologist has to follow landmarks when in the field, and if he is good for anything, he will endeavour to do the same when he is drawing conclusions from his facts and observations."

6

" By the way," said Baxter, " what made you take
up with such a curious subject as geology? It
seems to me to consist mainly of hard names and
dry details ; and, so far as I can judge, it doesn't
help one much in theology."

" Your question would take a deal of answering,"
I replied. " Geology has a great deal to do with
theology ; but if it had not, a preacher ought by
no means to limit his studies to what is technically
called theology. If he does, he will very likely
become a Dr. Dryasdust. I began to read geological
books long before I took to preaching, and my
early love has never faded. When a boy at
school I received Dr. Harris's *Pre-Adamite Earth*
for a prize, and I was so fascinated with its
marvellous stories of old-world life that the science
has kept hold of my imagination ever since. Your
ideas about it, I know, are very prevalent. I
remember a passage in Wordsworth's *Excursion*
which rather humorously describes the geologist :—

> 'You may trace him oft
> By scars which his activity has left
> Beside our roads and pathways—
> He who with pocket hammer smites the edge
> Of every luckless rock or stone that stands
> Before his sight by weather stains disguised,
> Or crusted o'er with vegetation thin,
> Nature's first growth, detaching by the stroke
> A chip or splinter—to resolve his doubts ;
> And with that ready answer satisfied,
> Doth to the substance give some barbarous name ;
> Then hurries on, or from the fragment picks
> His specimen.'

If the poet had lived to this day, he would have been amongst the first to recognize the value of geology, and to perceive its bearing upon some of the most vital problems of life and religion."

"But," said Baxter, "don't you think it would have been all the better for religion if there had never been any such thing as geology? I, of course, know nothing about the science, but one frequently hears it said that geologists deny the Bible statement that the world was created in six days, and that their doctrines would make our planet many millions of years old."

"I am afraid, my dear fellow, that many Christians misunderstand geologists, just as some geologists misrepresent the Bible. I think, however, the time is approaching when scientific men generally will see that the Christian religion does not necessarily make men narrow-minded and bigoted, and when there will not be a single Christian who will stand in dread of scientific inquiry and discovery. Now you must bear in mind that Moses does not assert that the world is only six thousand years old. It is doubtful whether he said that even the human race is that age. The chronology of the Pentateuch has been arranged with the utmost care, I know; but you are perfectly aware of the vast differences that exist amongst the various calculations, as, for example, those of Hales and Ussher. Geology, however, has not proved man to be much older than about six thousand years. The wild arithmetic of a few who are of rationalistic or atheistic tendencies, and who are ready to deny

the Bible statements, even without any scientific
authority, must not be taken as the deliberate and
final verdict of geologists. With regard to the
physical universe, the language of Moses harmonizes
perfectly with the belief in its enormous antiquity,
and Christians ought to feel grateful to geologists
for leading us out of the false interpretations which
for so many centuries have obscured the sacred
narrative. And if geology should, later on, make
it undeniable that the human race is of much
greater antiquity than we have been taught to
regard it, surely it is well for us to know what
the truth is, so that we may, in this respect also,
arrive at more accurate interpretations of the
Scriptures."

" But," said my friend, "supposing that our Bible
chronologies may be stretched a few thousand years
that would not meet the enormous demands of
geology, would it?"

" I don't say it is necessary to stretch our Scripture
chronology. As I have said, geology has not demonstrated that man is more than about six
thousand years of age. I can affirm this on the
authority of Sir J. W. Dawson, of Montreal, one of
the most reliable geologists of our time. But still,
I don't care to regard Moses as teaching that our
race is no older than six thousand years, for he does
nothing of the kind. Your difficulty, however, I
can clearly see, is not with regard to man's age,
but arises from the fact that there must have been
life on the earth, according to the evidence of fossils,
myriads of years before Adam was created."

" Precisely so. Creation is said in Genesis to
have occupied six days—the six days immediately
preceding man's appearance—and I really don't see
how that statement can be reconciled with what
our geologists hold concerning the antiquity of the
earth, and of plants and animals. This is why I
have looked upon geology with mistrust, and have
regarded it as atheistic in tendency and anti-
Scriptural in teaching."

" Still, my dear friend," said I, " you must admit
that it is better to know the truth than that we
should even pin our faith to the most venerable
writer if he is in error. You may depend upon it,
the evidence of geology will have to be as clear as
sunlight, and as undeniable as that two and two
make four, before the narrative which we regard as
divinely inspired is given up at the bidding of that
science. But you need be in no sort of fear, for
Moses is not in the least danger yet from geological
researches. In fact, Moses nowhere says the universe was made in six days of twenty-four hours ;
but, rightly viewed, his language prophetically
sanctions the modern geological doctrines on the
subject of the earth's antiquity. It is probable that
they who lived before Moses knew better than our
grandfathers what the truth of this matter is, but
the early traditions by the time of Moses had lost
something of their fulness, and hence the inspired
language which Moses wrote has all along been
misunderstood, to be more accurately explained in
our time as the result of geological studies. As
soon as ever the records of the rocks were ac-

curately deciphered, it was perceived that creation
must have occupied long ages, and theologians, put
upon the right scent, quickly saw that the Mosaic
use of the word ' day ' not only sanctioned, but even
demanded, its recent explanation as meaning indefinite duration, or uninterrupted time."

" But does not that interpretation imply the taking
of great liberties with the language of Scripture ? "

" Not at all," I answered. " The word ' day ' has
never been, nor is it now, used to denote just twenty-
four hours, except in a technical way and by an
accommodation of language. In common parlance
' day,' as you know, means the period of light as
distinguished from night. By general consent the
word is frequently applied to long and indefinite
periods. It is in this sense that Moses uses it in
Genesis, and, ·indeed, in other places. The first
' day ' was the first period in which light was
caused to shine on the darkness and confusion of
the earth's primary condition."

" Yes, but how does that explanation fit in to the
succeeding days of creation ? "

" Oh, perfectly well. The separation of the terrestrial from the atmospheric waters took place during
the second epoch—that is, the cooling earth had
become sufficiently low in temperature for water to
lie upon its surface instead of rising as vapour.
The gathering together of the seas in the depressions
of the earth, and the sprouting forth of lowly herbs,
occupied the third period, and during the fourth
the vapours had sufficiently condensed to allow of
the heavenly luminaries being visible, and becoming

signs for the division of day from night, and for the reckoning of seasons, days, and years. The creation of all such animals as inhabit the water or fly through the air is ascribed to the fifth epoch, while during the sixth land, animals, and man were made. You see, then, that the word 'day' is used of a time when as yet the sun did not 'divide the day from the night.' Besides, in this very chapter the word has several different significations. The first time it occurs it means 'light.' You remember it is said, 'God called the light Day.' In the very same verse it denotes both 'the evening and the morning'— that is, the period of confusion and of order. It is also used of the duration of light as affected by the sun. And in the second chapter of Genesis it is made to include the entire period of creation, and is used likewise to refer to the Divine rest or cessation from creation—that is, from that special manifestation of creative agency described by Moses ; and this rest has continued to our time. All through the Scriptures—and indeed in every other book— the word 'day' is used in this indefinite manner, and no one ever mistakes the meaning intended. The Mosaic use of it would never have been misconceived had men possessed the least knowledge of the condition of things during the ages which the word denotes in the Book of Genesis. I have not much doubt that Moses himself understood that the periods of creation were of indefinite duration, or he would not have chosen so elastic a word as 'day' to describe them, especially as he must have been conscious that he

was applying it to periods when as yet the sun
was not referred to."

"This is all new to me," said Baxter, with ani-
mation. "You see I have never been drawn out in
this direction before. But I begin to think I have
been labouring under very great delusions, and I
shall certainly look with more reverence on geology
henceforth, now that I see how valuable a handmaid
it is to the adequate understanding of the Mosaic
record of the creation."

"I am glad to hear you say that," I replied. "And
if ever you should set about the study of geology,
don't forget Dawson, and Dana, and Kingsley. You
will, of course, be obliged to read Lyell, and Geikie,
and Boyd Dawkins, but be sure you look at Hugh
Miller, Hitchcock, and Pye Smith. But, if you don't
care to go into the subject to any extent, let me
recommend you to read, at least, an admirable little
book, published by the Sunday School Union, on
The Creation."

"Do you really think this kind of reading would
help me at all in my preaching?"

"Decidedly I do. There are persons, I am aware,
who deride scientific study, but they are only those
who are densely ignorant of science. All scientific
knowledge is valuable to the preacher if he knows
how to keep it in its proper place. Many a chord
in the Bible has lain silent for ages, and might have
remained so for ever, had not science discovered it
and caused it to vibrate with sweet music."

We had by this time reached the cutting that
we were searching for, and, turning off the road,

hastened over two or three fields in the direction of
the grey escarpment which was visible at some little
distance ahead. On reaching it we found a lime
quarry of considerable size. We at once entered it,
and quietly surveyed the steep walls of rock of a
greyish white colour, mixed with bands or layers
of darker argillaceous shale, which rose up all
round us to a height of from thirty to forty feet.
We were completely shut off from the outer world,
and in the quarry intense stillness reigned.

" I can hardly expect you to enter into my feelings,"
said I to Baxter ; " but what a magnificent spectacle
this is to one who knows the history of these rocks !
These deposits tell, in language too plain to be
misunderstood, that over them once rolled the
great sea, and in every handful of that lime are
the gravestones of the former inhabitants of the
ocean which myriads of ages ago murmured here."

" Then this limestone," said my companion, " is
largely made up of the shells of creatures which used
to live in the sea, is it ? "

" Yes. Most limestones have been deposited in
deep seas. This particular quarry belongs to what
are called the Wenlock beds, which are nearly two
thousand feet thick, and are crowded with organic
remains. You may imagine the length of time it
must have taken for that thickness of lime to be
slowly deposited by the continual dropping of shells
and the gradual labours of tiny corals. Above the
Wenlock series are the Ludlow beds, about two
thousand feet thick, while below are the Woolhope
formations, three thousand feet in thickness. These,

with some others, constitute what are called the
Upper Silurian strata.   Below are many thousands
of feet of Lower Silurian, Cambrian, and Pre-
Cambrian formations ; while above are the enormous
deposits of Old Red Sandstone, Coal, Millstone
Grit, New Red Sandstone, the Oolites, Chalk, and
numerous other kinds of rock and clay, all laid by
decaying forests or by the accumulation of animal
remains.   Now, perhaps, you can form an idea of
the sort of evidence which has led geologists to give
up the belief that our globe is only some few thousands of years old."

"Indeed I can," said Baxter ; "but, to tell the
truth, you almost take away my breath."

"Oh," said I laughingly, "out of pity for you I have
told you next to nothing of the wonders casketed
in the rocks ; you can't digest geological strong
meat yet.   But let us get to work, for we shall find
the time go quickly."

The first thing to be done was to sketch the
adjacent district and to draw a diagram of the
section before us.   Then marking down the various
thicknesses and directions of the bands of stone,
and the angles which the beds made with the floor,
measurements which are known technically as the
dip, strike, downthrow, and so on, all the prelimi-
naries were finished and work was begun in earnest.
I asked Baxter to grope about wherever he liked,
and if he came across anything that looked interesting among the débris to bring it to me.   To
some people our occupation would have seemed
toilsome drudgery ; but, to those who are trained

to understand only a tithe of what they witness, there are few things so exhilarating or so worthy of occupying the hours of a holiday as fossil-hunting in a favourable spot.

After some hours spent in climbing, jumping, rolling slabs and blocks of stone over, hammering and chiselling, brightened by snatches of conversation, we proposed a rest for the double purpose of eating our luncheon and talking over our " finds."

Various specimens of coral had been secured ; for the Wenlock limestone is in many parts almost a mass of coral, probably an ancient coral reef, like those which stretch for hundreds of miles in the Southern Seas, whose wondrous history Charles Darwin so graphically wrote. What we call coral is really the skeleton or solid support of the tiny creatures which formed the substance. Mr. Darwin believed that coral islands and reefs are gradually built up by colonies of minute animals, until by alterations in the level of the sea the structure rises above the surface of the water, and then, by the drifting of seeds and in other ways, vegetation sprouts out, trees grow, and at length man himself finds a home upon the island which has been formed.

Darwin's theory, like all others, has had to be tried by the test of accumulating facts and knowledge, and, as some affirm, is found wanting. I have not space now for even a brief account of the controversy which this question has originated, but I shall deal with it in another chapter when I come to write more exclusively upon corals. Let it suffice to say at present that it would be no discredit to Darwin even if his theory, which was received with almost universal admiration at first, should be found not to cover the whole of the phenomena concerned ; and he himself, I am sure, would be amongst the first, were he alive, to admit the validity of evidence that seemed to be true and reliable ; yet I cannot help feeling that after all his explanation does account for many of the facts of the case.

Montgomery, in his *Pelican Island* has described this coral fabric as

> "The mausoleum of its architects,
> Still dying upwards as their labours closed ;
> Slime their material, but the slime was turned
> To adamant by their petrific touch ;
> Frail were their frames, ephemeral their lives—
> Their masonry imperishable."

There were also several stone-lilies (Encrinites), with their many-jointed stalks, and which sometimes may be discovered with their flower-shaped cups surmounting the stalks. The separated joints of the stalks, each of which is a distinct animal, have some resemblance to beads ; hence, in different parts of the country, they are known as " St. Cuthbert's beads " and " wheel stones." Like the coral, this substance is really made up of the skeletons of the creatures which once existed in it, and so enormous was the number of them that whole beds of limestone owe their formation almost entirely to them— as, for instance, the encrinital limestone.

Nothing else invited special remark except the lamp-shells. These are bivalves, and are called

technically Brachiopoda. They differ from the more
ordinary types of bivalves, such as mussels, oysters,
etc. (Lamellibranchiata), in being always equal-sided
and never quite equivalvular—*i.e.*, the two shells
are symmetrical, but not of equal size. The old
naturalists called them *lampades*, or lamp-shells,
from their fancied resemblance to the antique lamps
of symmetrical form, whose wick corresponded to
the pedicle, or footstalk, by which the creature in a
later stage of development attaches itself to some
submarine object.

After some further talk about our specimens, we
resumed our hunt. Baxter stopped me in a moment
or two, however, by saying, " I am not quite clear
about the way in which these rocks, which, you say,
were formed at the bottom of the sea, have become
elevated and removed so far from the ocean. I
have been puzzling over that problem ever since
we got into the quarry. Do you think you could
explain it a little more simply for my dull comprehension ? "

" It is probable," I replied, " that volcanic agency
had a great deal to do with the matter in this
particular place. If you will just step up here
where I have been at work, you will get a' tolerably
good view of the surrounding district, and you will
perhaps be able to make out that it is roughly conical.
Sir Roderick Murchison, whose magnificent work
Siluria is by far the best geological guide for
this part of the country, is of opinion that this
locality forms the crater of a gigantic extinct volcano,
which has been worn down by the action of water

and climate to what it now is. Enormous submarine volcanoes, such as must have been in almost continual action when the earth's crust was perhaps thinner than now, would speedily pour out masses of material extensive enough to alter the level of the ocean bed, and cause its waters to drain off to other parts of the land. Extraordinary changes in the distribution of land and sea have taken place within historic times, and even during our own lifetime, from the same or similar causes."

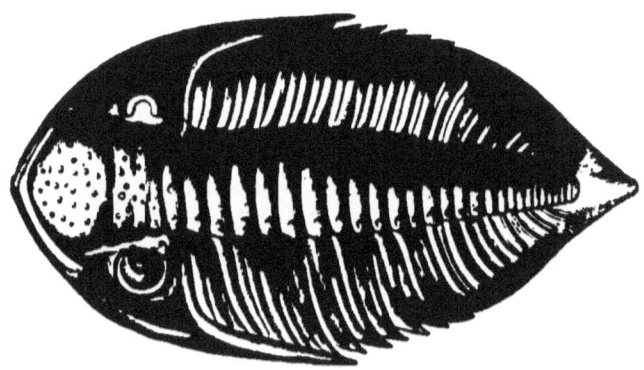

FIG. 16.—Trilobite (*Phacops caudatus*).

When we had been at work for another hour, Baxter suddenly cried out, "What in the world is this? I think I have discovered something at last." Taking the piece of limestone from his hand, and looking at it, I saw at once he had managed to knock out of the rock with his rude hammer of stone a very valuable fossil.

"Well, you are a lucky dog," I said. "You have actually got the greater part of a trilobite; the Fates evidently intend you to be a geologist."

"A trilobite? I think I have heard of that creature before."

'I dare say you have. It is often referred to in discussions on Design and Evolution. Trilobites belong to the same animal group (Crustacea) as the lobster. They are found in works far older than even these ancient Wenlock strata; indeed, they are amongst the oldest inhabitants of our globe. Although they became extinct many ages ago, for they do not occur in any rocks newer than the Carboniferous, yet so perfectly have they been preserved, and in such vast numbers, that it is possible to study their structure, even to the minutest detail, from their fossil remains. Their external covering is divided into three lobes, and it is this feature which has originated their name; for trilobite, as you know, means three-lobed. They vary greatly in size, some, like the Olenus, being as small as a pea, and others attaining to a length of several feet. These interesting creatures can be traced through about twenty metamorphic stages. Dr. Buckland, in his famous "Bridgewater Treatise," pointed out that the same modification of the organ of vision is found in this earliest Crustacean as in some living representatives of this group; hence, the mutual relations between light and the eye must have been the same in those remote ages as at the present day. Any argument for the doctrine of Evolution, therefore, which is based on a supposed change of environment since those primeval ages, is certainly weakened by the evidence which the trilobite's eye furnishes. The trilobite, moreover, could swim and burrow in the sand ; it was protected with an almost impregnable case, while its head was covered with hard shields, and it could roll itself up in a stone-like ball when pursued by its foes. How is it that such a highly organised animal, with an eye as perfect as that of the modern insect, consisting of hundreds of lenses, with a structure so eminently adapted to its modes of life, should appear at its best at the very dawn of its existence in the Cambrian age, and go on gradually deteriorating until it died out in the Carboniferous age ? Is this the survival of the fittest ? The difficulty has, of course, been grappled with by Darwinians, but it has not been utterly explained away."

"Then you are not an evolutionist," said my friend.

"I can only answer that question by saying Yes and No. There is no word in the English vocabulary so abused as the word evolution. It is used for education, for growth, for the processes of nature's laws, and for the transmutations by which the original nebula out of which our globe is said to have been produced has resulted in the highest animal forms, including even man. It implies creation by formative laws, under the superintendency of a Deity, and it is put in the place of God by those who are atheistically inclined. You see, then, how difficult it is for me to say whether I am an evolutionist or not. Then, you must not forget that every man who declares himself an anti-evolutionist is at once laughed at as an

ignoramus by the more ill-mannered of the other
side, and, as one doesn't care to be thought a fool,
I prefer to ask my scientific inquisitors to furnish
me with a careful definition of what they mean
by evolution, by which piece of subtlety I mostly
manage to evade an answer. I have really tried
honestly to find out what is meant by evolution,
and have left no influential book unexamined ; but I
find there are almost as many opinions as there are
evolutionists, and so I have come to the conclusion
that there are no real evolutionists, but that all
who are so styled are simply on their way to the
truth which they have not yet reached. The
extreme forms of evolutionism which were rampant
a score of years ago are fast dying out, and perhaps
you and I may live to see the very word almost
forgotten. Already the myth of spontaneous
generation is given up, even by Haeckel ; and,
moreover, man is declared by all ' who are competent to judge '—as Professor Huxley is fond of
saying when writing polemically—as being of an
order distinct from, and higher than, the rest of
creation. Geology and zoology prove nothing yet,
except that we need to revise our notions about
species, and that our natural history classifications
have; been made upon wrong principles, so that
varieties have been elevated into more important
groups. There is no ground for believing that all
types of plants and animals have developed from
one archetype, or that both sexes have, by ordinary
processes, evolved from one individual. The whole
question of development and degeneration is at

7

present in a chaotic state, and they are the wisest
who weigh evidence and suspend judgment."

This valuable find whetted the appetite of my
friend, and now the only thing he regretted was
that he had not come furnished with hammer and
chisel, instead of having to call in to his aid the
hereditary instincts which are said to have come
down to us from our stone-age progenitors. So
absorbed were we both that several hours passed
by without weariness, and I was quite astonished
when at length, looking at my watch, I found that
we had been in that quarry no less than eight hours.
We had now to select our specimens, label and
describe them, wrap up in paper the more fragile
ones, and pack them in the leathern receptacle
which I had brought for that purpose. Besides
the corals and stone-lilies, we bagged several portions of trilobites, perfect specimens being rarely
captured ; a large number of Molluscan species
(shell-fish), such as the lamp-shells, the beautifully striated Orthis, the graceful Strophomena,
the Atrypa, and the Rhynchonella, and a few other
things.

We beguiled our rather long walk home with
conversation on the topic to which Baxter had
already referred. We talked on until we reached
our respective abodes, thankful for rest and re-
freshment after so long and diligent a tour, and
both, I believe, satisfied that we had spent as
cheerful and profitable a day as any of the holiday-
makers that we saw flitting here and there around
us. As for Baxter, he has since then become a

confirmed and incurable fossil-hunter, and, as he is not restricted by the exigencies of the itinerant system, he has been able to collect quite a small museum of specimens, all which dire events he attributes to the conversation and exploits of that bright summer day when we spent together those busy, happy hours in a Quarry.

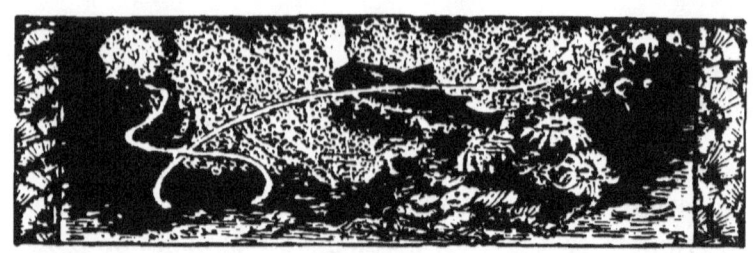

VII.

ST. HILDA'S SNAKE-STONES.

"On the pavement lay
Carved stones of the abbey-ruin in the park,
Huge Ammonites, and the first bones of Time."

TENNYSON.

ERY curious, and sometimes exceedingly amusing, are the experiences of the man who travels about in search of natural history specimens. Whether it be for insects or shells or fossils, he soon finds not only material for his cabinets, but also an abundance of folk-lore of a most interesting character, of which every branch of science has its store. I very well remember, during one of my geological tours in the north of England, being invited to look at the collection of an old pensioner, who had won quite a reputation in the village for being a geologist. On going to the house I was at once taken into the garden, where the bulk of the specimens had been arranged as ornaments on miniature grottoes, and in the crevices of larg

lumps of cork. This did not look very promising,
but I held my peace, and waited and observed.
One after another of the old man's curiosities was
pointed out to me, and among them were shown
with great gusto a number of "petrified snakes,"
as he called them. I had already made the
discovery that the old man was more of an artist
than a naturalist, and was quite impressed with
the taste and accuracy of some of the heads cast
in clay which here and there lay about, and which
he had moulded with his own hands. I suspected
at once, therefore, what his petrified snakes would
turn out to be, and so did not pitch my hopes
very high. When we came to them, I found, as
I had already surmised would be the case, that
his fossil snakes were Ammonites, whose curled
shells are so suggestive of a coiled snake. To
complete the delusion, and to evince the old man's
belief that they really were vipers in stone, he
had affixed to the end of the coil a snake's head
of clay. It required a good deal of talk to convince
the old gentleman that the objects were not snake-
stones, but merely the shells of creatures very
similar to the recent Nautilus. It was at Whitby
where this notion first took its rise, and for ages
it was held as an undoubted fact that St. Hilda
had transformed all the snakes into stone. Sir
Walter Scott, in his *Marmion* has given poetical
form to this old legend in lines that are familiar
enough to most geologists, and to many visitors
to romantic Whitby. I quoted them to the old
man :

" The nuns of Whitby told
How, of the countless snakes, each one
Was turned into a coil of stone,
   When holy Hilda prayed.
Themselves within their sacred bound
Their stony coils had often found."

For ages these beautiful fossils have been the
objects of superstitious reverence on account of
their resemblance to coiled-up serpents and snakes.
In Egypt this was especially the case in earlier
times. The Brahmins treasured them up in costly
caskets and offered sacrifices to them, while the
Hindoos also rendered to them a sort of worship.

Next to Whitby, there is perhaps no place more
favourable for the study of Ammonites than Lincoln,
and it is there that I first felt the fascination of them.
Any one who will take the trouble to visit Swan's
brickyard will find a splendid section of Liassic clay
exposed, clearly definable into three of those remarkable zones with which the Liassic deposits have been
divided, each one containing its characteristic Ammonite. Just as Europe might be divided into
sections each with its own type of man, or as the
seashore can be marked out into regions characterised by different sorts of seaweeds, so the whole of
the vast beds that make up the Liassic formation
are arranged in divisions or zones, in each of which
are types of Ammonites scarcely found elsewhere.
In this brickyard, where the Upper Lias is exposed,
the three zones visible are those characterised by
Ammonites bifrons, A. communis, and *A. serpentinus.*

Another pit lies to the south of the river gorge,
and formed quite a picturesque foreground to the

view from one of the windows at the back of my house. Here the Middle Lias may be examined; and the lovely *A. margaritatus,* of pearly lustre, along with *A. capricornis,* of ruder aspect, supply the standards of the zones. The deeper portions of the Lias may nearly all be seen by the enthusiastic collector who will go out to two or three of the villages south of Lincoln, such as Waddington and Leadenham. It is certainly very remarkable that the respective Ammonites of these closely related

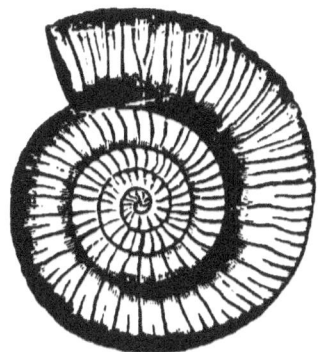  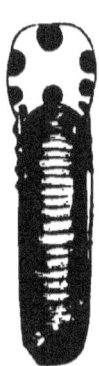

FIG. 17.—*A. communis.*   FIG. 18.—Side view.

zones should present such differences. It is one of those curious and profound problems which the geologist is continually meeting with. For those who may wish a more detailed and systematic account of these zones, I may mention that a complete list of them, formed by a comparison of the Liassic beds of the whole country, is given on p. 786 of Geikie's larger *Geology*. Mr. Etheridge has shown that these zones hold good for the whole of the Secondaries throughout Asia, Europe, and America.

I have just said that the Ammonite is closely related to the modern Nautilus.   In order to obtain, therefore, an idea of what the animal which inhabited these wonderful shells was like, we cannot do better than examine a Nautilus, an illustration of which is given.   No Ammonites have existed in our seas since the close of the Secondary epoch of geology, but

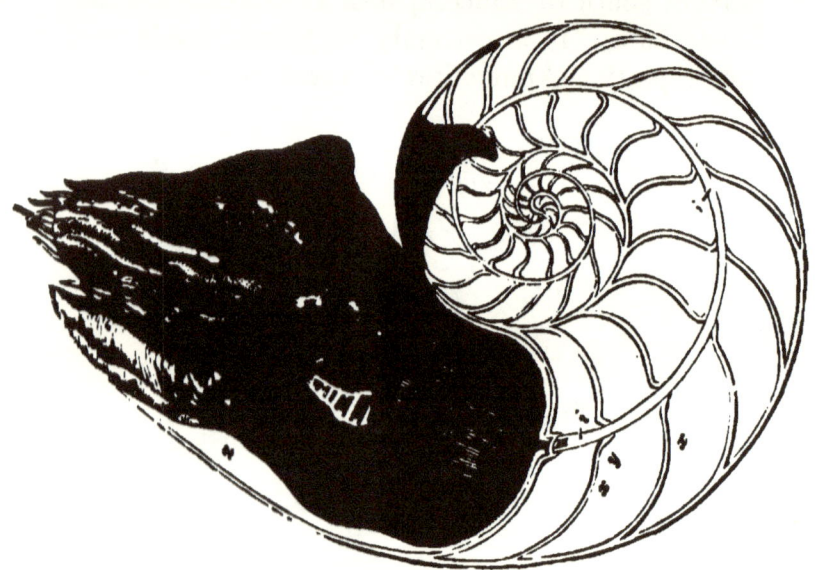

Fig. 19.—Pearly Nautilus.

there is no reason for doubting that the Nautilus is the modern representative of this ancient and noble race, which once crowded the waters of our globe.

Although the shell of the Nautilus is seen to consist of many chambers, yet the entire animal is confined to the last of these, which, in consequence, is called the body-chamber.   From this chamber the animal can protrude its head at will.   The chambers are constructed one after the other as the animal's growth demands more room. The deserted chambers are then walled off by a curved pearly division or septum, the communication between the chambers being, however, kept up by means of a membranous tube, called the siphuncle (*i*), which is continued throughout the whorls of the shell.

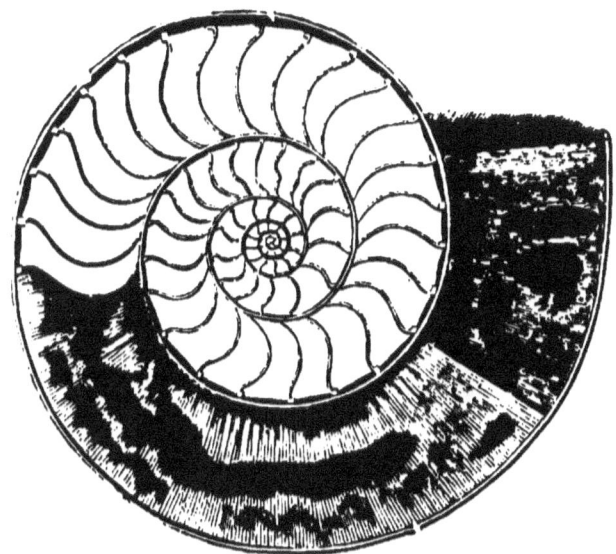

Fig. 20.—Section of shell of Ammonite.

In the Nautilus this siphuncle runs through the central part of the chambers, whereas in Ammonites it lies on the outside or dorsal portion. The creature has a heart, four pyramid-shaped branchiæ or gills, two large eyes attached by short stalks to the sides of the head, with various organs concerned in reproduction. Its tentacles are prehensile, and are useful in procuring food, two of them being fused together so as to form a strong hood with which to close the shell. There is a nervous system, consisting mainly of two masses or ganglia, protected partially by a cartilaginous plate which we may regard as a kind of rudimentary skull. It is clear then that the creature is by no means a lowly organised one ; indeed, it is placed at the very top of the Mollusca, which are only a short step behind the Vertebrates. The function of the chambers of the shell is probably that of enabling the animal to alter its specific gravity, but what are the precise uses of the siphuncle does not seem to be understood.

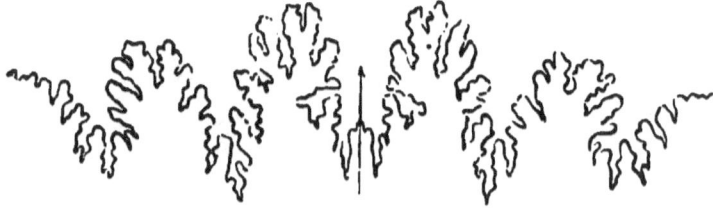

FIG. 21.—Foliation of Ammonite chambers.

The chief differences between a Nautilus and an Ammonite have to do with the walls that divide the chambers. In the case of the former the divisions or *septa* are simple, and where they join the shell the lines are plain. But the *septa* of Ammonites have frilled edges of many patterns. These patterns form very beautiful traceries on the exterior shells of Ammonites. A representation of one of these diversified patterns is given (Fig. 21).

It is worthy of remark, too, that the Nautilus family made its appearance in the waters of our globe long before Ammonites existed, and, indeed, many of its genera had already become extinct before the true Ammonites began to exist ; while the Nautilus still survives, although Ammonites have been absolutely extinct for ages.

As a help in the identification of specimens it

FIG. 22.—*A. bifrons.*   FIG. 23.—Side view of *A. bifrons.*

may be as well to present illustrations of a few of the commoner species.

Ammonites bifrons (Fig. 22) occurs in considerable numbers in the Upper Lias. Although appearing to characterise one of the zones at Lincoln, this is not found to be the case elsewhere. The shell has a sickle-shaped sculpturing on the sides, and the body chamber occupies about one-half of the first whorl or spiral.

A. communis (Fig. 17) is very plentiful in the Middle and Upper Lias, and gives its name to one of the Liassic zones. Its shell ornamentation consists of rings, the side view showing portions of these circular lines lying parallel with each other.

A. obtusus (Fig. 24) is a characteristic fossil of the Lower Lias. It has a keel on the back of the shell with radiating ribs along the sides. The body chamber is large, occupying more than one complete whorl.

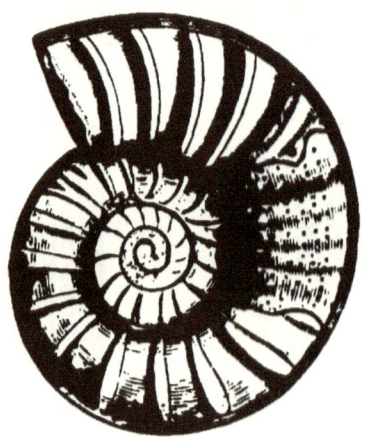

FIG. 24.—*A. obtusus.*   FIG. 25.—Side view.

So far I have mentioned only Liassic Ammonites, but they occur all through the Secondaries, that is, the Lias, the Oolites, and the Chalk. One of the commonest, as well as one of the most beautiful, of these fossils is *A. lautus* (Fig. 26), from the Cretaceous series. The Gault beds in this series, seen so well at Folkestone, are crowded with Ammonites of almost every conceivable pattern. They vary remarkably in size, some, like *A. lautus*, being less than half an inch in diameter, while in the Oolites there are species which measure a yard across.

What the precise position of the Ammonite is in the chain of life cannot be definitely settled. The modifications through which these creatures have passed can only be guessed at by observing minute changes in the shells. Such changes are said to have been observed as proceeding from the outer whorl more and more towards the centre, as geological time rolled on. The earliest Ammonites were smooth, later on they had ribs, and still later

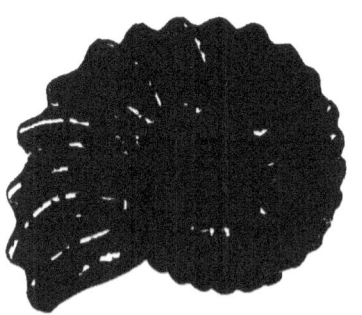

FIG. 26.—*A. lautus.*

spines appeared. The line of descent is usually traced backwards through Goniatites with simpler shell, and onwards, as has already been indicated, to the Nautilus. But the line is confused and broken, and the Nautilus, which is regarded as the lingering scion of a great race, seems destined to die out.

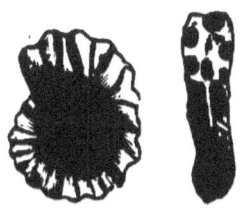

FIG. 27.—*A. varicosus* and side view.

VIII.

A VISIT TO GREENWICH OBSERVATORY.

" And for the heaven's wide circuit, let it speak
The Maker's high magnificence; Who built
So spacious, and His line stretched out so far,
That man may know he dwells not in his own."

MILTON.

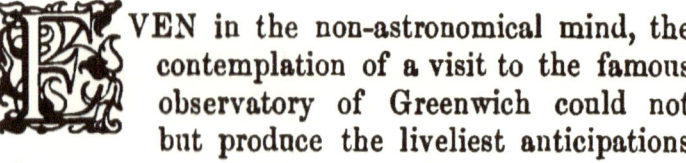VEN in the non-astronomical mind, the contemplation of a visit to the famous observatory of Greenwich could not but produce the liveliest anticipations of pleasure and instruction. When, therefore, an arrangement had been made for a few of us to go down to that mysterious workshop of envied students of the skies, the hour was looked forward to with great and eager hopes. Being at that time the happy possessor of a three-inch telescope equatorially mounted, and having dabbled in the allied pursuits of photography and spectroscopy, I naturally cherished large expectations of adding to my scanty stock of knowledge in regard to these most attractive branches of astronomical science.

We none of us, of course, believed that we were going to see the most advanced instruments which

the astronomical world has to show, for most
Englishmen understand, and are ashamed to confess
it, that even Greenwich is behind the age in the
matter of apparatus, though certainly not as respects
men. But talent, ingenuity, industry, though they
can accomplish vast things, cannot supply the lack
of the highest and most elaborate machinery and
optical powers.

It may be as well to say here that telescopes are
mainly of two kinds. There is the refractor, through
which the star or other object is looked at directly.
There is also the reflector, through which the star
itself is not actually seen, but its image is reflected
from a large mirror or *speculum* up the tube, and is
magnified by the eye-piece apparatus. The first refractor was the one invented by Galileo, and through
it he saw, probably for the first time in human
history, the satellites of Jupiter. The largest refractor in the world is the one lately erected at the
Lick Observatory on Mount Hamilton, in California,
the object glass of which is thirty-six inches
across. The Russians have the next best refracting
telescope, that of Professor Struve of Polkowa, the
diameter of which is thirty inches. The Vienna
refractor is twenty-seven inches, the Harvard College
one is twenty-six inches, and then comes Mr. R. S.
Newall's, lately presented to Cambridge, which
measures twenty-five inches, and was at the time
of its construction the largest in the world.

The finest reflector in the world is the one of
which everybody has heard, that belonging to Lord
Rosse, of Parsonstown, in Ireland, whose speculum

is six feet in diameter. But in regard to definition, the diameter of a reflector must not be compared with the diameter of a refractor, the latter being in every way superior. So that we are obliged to admit that so far our astronomers have not been at all on an advantageous footing in comparison with several other nations in regard to the mechanical and optical appliances of the observatory.

But although our Greenwich establishment is not so splendidly equipped as others, yet it remains to be seen whether the more imposing instruments possessed by our transatlantic cousins will answer to the expectations formed concerning them ; and, even if they do, it will be long before Greenwich will be put into the shade. The records of its work are a magnificent testimony to England's enterprise and industry, and, notwithstanding our changeful skies and the niggardliness which our Government has usually shown in regard to science, it must be many years before any other country can show such results as are chronicled in the archives of Greenwich, or such a noble line of astronomical heroes as England can boast of in Flamsteed, Newton, Halley, the Herschels, Adams, and Airy.

On our way down to the Observatory,—up, as one or two of our stouter companions found it to be towards: the end of our journey,—we beguiled the time with talk about ancient astronomies, the Pyramid observatories, the astronomical structures of Benares and Delhi, the Ptolemaic system, the incidents relating to Tycho Brahé and Copernicus

and other subjects concerned in the development of
astronomy.

Permission to go through the Observatory had
been kindly granted by the Astronomer Royal, and
one of his assistants, E. W. Maunder, Esq., F.R.A.S.,
accompanied the party, explaining the various instruments and their uses. Mr. Maunder interspersed
his talk with some interesting references to the
origin and history of the place. The Observatory
was founded in 1675 by Charles II., Flamsteed
being appointed " our astronomical observator," at
a munificent salary of £100 a year, out of which
he was to find his own instruments ! At that time
astronomy was to the bulk of the people very little
more than astrology, and to the rustics of Greenwich Flamsteed was a kind of chief horoscopist.
It is related that an old woman went to him to
obtain help in finding a lost basket. The astronomer gravely drew some circles on the ground,
and then pointed with his stick in a certain
direction. To his great surprise, the woman soon
came back to tell him he was right, and he found
himself famous ; but he determined to practise
astrology no more, even in jest.

Flamsteed, having to provide his own apparatus,
naturally enough thought he had the right to all
the results of his researches; but the Royal Society,
backed by Newton, claimed them as public property,
and even went so far as to seize by force all the
records that were treasured up in the Observatory.
This caused dissension between Newton and Flamsteed, and it is not impossible that the papers of

the astronomer had something to do with the discovery of gravitation. This great law, like many other wonderful things, seems not to have been discovered solely by the labours of one man, but it was certainly Newton, not Flamsteed nor Descartes, who first gave it scientific form, and gave such mathematical demonstration of it as has placed it for ever beyond dispute.

The first instrument seen was the great transit telescope, which by means of its wonderful spider lines enables the observer to determine the instant at which celestial bodies cross the meridian. The telescope is so mounted that its optical axis may move only in the plane of the meridian, and the dome above it can be opened to the sky in the same plane. So delicate are the movements of this apparatus that a change of a few feet in the adjustment of the mercury vessel will, to the confusion of John Hampden and all other flat-earth theorists, indicate the rotundity of the earth within that short space. Connected with the transit instrument, but in another room, is the chronograph, which registers on a revolving barrel covered with prepared paper the manipulations of the observer at the telescope. Here a very curious fact was pointed out. Different observers see and transmit phenomena in different periods of time. As a psychologist would say, cerebration varies in different individuals. By a subtle arrangement these variations of mental activity can be measured, and when the amount of variation, or "personal equation," is known for a certain person, his observations can be compared

with those of others. When will it be possible
to obtain a "personal equation" that will enable us
to reconcile the differences which prevail amongst
men in their views of truth? The astronomer is
to be envied by the moralist.

Then the equatorial of small degree was seen,
and after it the standard clock which gives time
to the world. Every day at one o'clock the great
ball drops, but, alas! it cannot rise till it is wound
up by a windlass turned by hand. Some day,
when the price of a hundred-ton gun can be spared,
this may be done automatically.

The altazimuth instrument enables the observer
to sweep any meridian of the sky. It is used
mostly for watching the moon, and the dome over
it opens at any point by means of machinery.
To sailors these observations are of the utmost
importance, for, with the astronomer's results before
him in the Nautical Almanac, the moon becomes
a kind of hand upon the giant dial of the sky, of
which the figures are the stars, and he can thus
ascertain his whereabouts in any part of the world.

The great equatorial telescope is the largest
instrument at Greenwich. Its object glass is a
little more than a foot across. What a pigmy
compared with those mighty instruments possessed
by our enlightened transatlantic cousins! Perhaps
some princely Lick will one day give England a
refractor with a diameter of three feet; or, better
still, we may some time be able to sell an ironclad
for the purpose. There is, however, we are glad
to state, a twenty-eight inch refractor being now

constructed, which, if not already in its place, soon
will be ; but even this splendid instrument will
leave England behind America and Russia in the
matter of telescopes. There is a piece of mechanism
in this room by means of which the object-glass
of the telescope can be taken out, cleaned, and
restored to its cell, without being touched by a
finger. A triumph of mechanical skill, it almost
seemed to live. This equatorial is used by Mr.
Maunder for spectroscopic work, and the visitors
were gratified by seeing the solar spectrum through
the six-inch spectroscope. Faint and incomplete
though it was by reason of the obscurity of the
sky, yet what a beautiful vision it was, and how
the spectacle threw one's thoughts back through
the wonderful stages of the history of solar physics
to the time when Newton in his dark room first
stood entranced before the analysis of the sunbeams
which were thrown upon the screen by his rude
prism !

The equatorial is worked by a wonderful water
clock, whose curious S-shaped turbine, by the
action of the water, sets up mechanical movements
that keep the telescope upon the star, notwithstanding its apparent motion.

There were also chronometers in scores, thermo-
meters for the registration of maximum and
minimum heat and dew-point, barometers, glass
globes for measuring the quantity of sunshine,
which looked as if they had not had much to do
lately ; photographic apparatus, chiefly for the
purpose of recording the history of the sun, for—

more unfortunate than most of us—he has to submit to have his portrait taken at least twice a day ; and, last of all, the reflecting telescope, whose speculum is only a third of the mighty mirror of Lord Rosse's instrument at Parsonstown.

All these great and curious things having been seen, Mr. Maunder received the thanks of his visitors. They dispersed, some to the pleasant Thames, down which they had found their way to Greenwich, and others to the less romantic but speedier track of iron, all carrying with them happy memories of this pleasant and instructive visit to the greatest astronomical centre of the world.

IX.

MARVELS OF THE POND.

" There is no great and no small
To the Soul that maketh all ;
And where it cometh, all things are ;
And it cometh everywhere."

EMERSON.

IF one were to be asked what creature occupies about the middle position in regard to size of the whole assemblage of animal life, perhaps an answer would be given which would somewhat surprise those who had not given the matter considerable attention. A cat would be thought by some to be not a very bad guess ; others might venture to descend as low in the scale as a mouse. But even the smallest of these would be many thousand times above the mark. We should probably be far more correct in taking the tiny house-fly as standing midway, in respect of bulk, between the huge elephant and those minute animals which the microscope reveals. And yet it is not a libel on mankind to say that the bulk of us are absolutely ignorant of almost every creature smaller than a fly. How startling to be told that, with only a comparatively few exceptions, man knows nothing at all about nearly one half of creation ! This realm, over which dominion was given to him "in the beginning," has not even been explored, save by an adventurous observer here and there.

In this chapter I want to give a few glimpses, at any rate, of this almost boundless region ; and to do so I shall have to describe organisms that no human eye can examine without optical aid.

We will make our way to some neighbouring pond where there is some kind of plant life, and with muslin net and collecting bottle will secure some of the mixed growing and decomposing vegetable matter that lies tangled together in the water. Or, if we keep an aquarium, it will only be necessary to place under the magic lens a minute spray of the weed that we may have there, or simply take a drop or two of the water and put it into the live box for inspection. There will at once start into vision all sorts and sizes of active organisms—round, oval, linear, while some have most bewitching forms of fairy-like beauty. In general, these living things are called *Infusoria*. The name originated from the fact that they usually abounded in infusions of vegetable matter. Indeed, if a few wisps of hay be put into a jar of rain or pond water and kept a day or two in a warm place, there will be found a number of these interesting creatures, and the more offensive the water becomes the more likely it is to contain some of the objects I am going to describe.

It may be as well to say that the word *Infusoria*

is not now regarded as a very scientific one, although
it has given a title to several highly scientific
volumes, such as Pritchard's magnificent *History
of the British Infusoria.* The term did very well
while hardly anything was known about the structure and affinities and development of the organisms;
but now that nearly all of them have been minutely
studied by microscopists, and their habits and life-
history thoroughly explained, they have to be
separated widely from one another in any accurate
zoological scale. In those days almost every tiny
thing that could swim about, even the spores of
mosses and ferns, and the zoospores of seaweeds,
were set down as animalcules, but we know better
now.

Well, we will begin with the lowliest of them,
the Amœba. It is not easy to detect it, unless one
knows what to look for. But do you see those
glairy, gum-like patches that seem to lie motionless
on the glass? Those are amœbæ. And they are
not motionless. Look well, and keep your eye
steadily fixed upon one of them. You will see that
it is not only not motionless, but it is never
still. Why, it was actually named after the old
mythical prophet Proteus, who never retained the
same form. It is now called amœba, which means
that it is ever changing. As you gaze at it you
will see how it slowly puts out a sort of limb from
some part of its body, which gradually twines itself
around some speck of food, and then draws back the
newly-made limb into the mass of its body, bringing
the tiny meal with it. Or it may pour its body by

a very curious process after the limb, and so manages to crawl about. It has no legs or arms, but it makes them as required. Neither has it any mouth, but it can manufacture one at any spot. As for a stomach, well, it is all stomach, for it takes in food all over. These limbs are usually called pseudopodia,

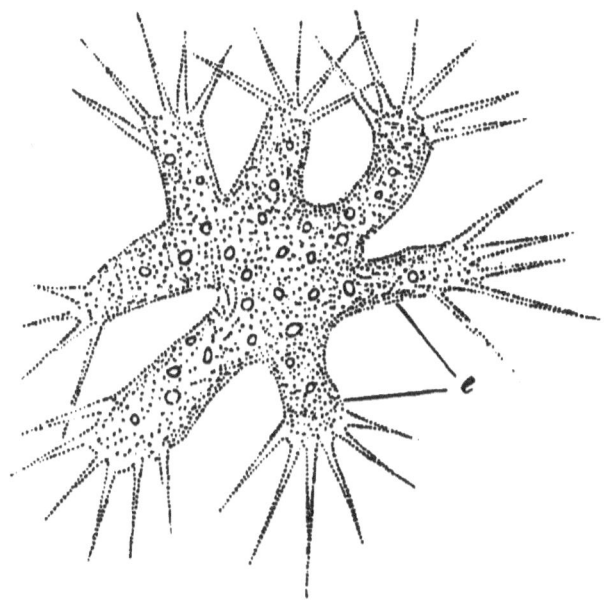

FIG. 28.—*Amœba.*

false feet, and consist of protoplasm, just the sort of stuff you and I are made of, if we go back to the original elements of the human body.

Imagine an amœba with a tiny shell, and you have one of those minute foraminifera whose long labours in the sea have done so much to build up the thousands of feet of chalk cliffs of our shores ;

or put it into a flinty skeleton, and it becomes a polycystin ; or range a mass of them together, and build around them walls and girders of flint, and a sponge is the result. The jelly animal is the same in every case, and all these agree in having no special limbs, any portion of the body fulfilling, in turn, the functions of arms, legs, mouth, or stomach. It is clear then that we are dealing with the lowest forms of animal life, and all the creatures just enumerated—amœba, foraminifera, polycystins, sponge —are grouped together in one large sub-kingdom, called Protozoa, which, as the name imports, stands on the lowest rung of the zoological ladder.

For more precise details respecting the structure of amœba we · had better look at Nicholson's *Zoology*. We learn there that the body of this animal is composed of gelatinous sarcode, and can be separated, theoretically at least, into an outer transparent layer, termed the " ectosarc " or " ectoplasm," and an inner layer, granular and mobile, called the " endosarc " or " endoplasm." It is the outer layer which constructs the pseudopodia, while the inner layer contains the nucleus, a spherical vesicle which contracts and expands with something approaching to regularity, and certain other cavities of a temporary nature called vacuoles. These are the only appearances of anything like organs that can be detected, and there are no traces whatever of nervous structure. The animal reproduces itself in the beautifully simple way of merely dividing itself into two.

Now we will take from our gatherings a tiny bit of the pond weed, of which there is a quantity lying in a tangled mass in our jar, or waving in delicate filaments towards the surface. Having placed it in a small trough or live-cage, we had better examine it first with an inch objective. Here is something worth a good long look. It is a tiny transparent object which seems to be moored to a twig, and is surmounted by a couple of wheel-like organs which appear to be incessantly revolving. It is at once pronounced to be a Rotifer, or wheel-animalcule.

Having found it, we proceed to examine it with a rather higher power. Suppose we use a half-inch lens. We can make the change in a moment, for our nose-piece is one in which three objectives can be screwed, and all that we have to do is to give a slight turn to this nose-piece and the half-inch is in position at once.

FIG. 29.
Rotifer vulgaris.

We have now a spectacle that, if one has never seen it before, is sure to be pronounced one of the most beautiful and curious ever beheld. Here are the wheels apparently turning round with astonishing rapidity, and just under them is a gizzard actively at work. These wheels are not really turning round, but they are made up of a circle of fine hairs, called cilia, which are lashing the water in quick succession, and that begets the illusion of revolution. If our eye-lashes were whipping the air in a similar fashion, it would really seem as if the eye was rotating. By the constant play of these cilia, the water in their neighbourhood is kept in a state of agitation, and multitudes of minute objects are brought by the miniature whirlpools within reach of the creature's mouth. Some of them are evidently rejected, for they fly away, while others may be seen to go into the hungry maw of the animal.

A very slight inspection is enough to show that the rotifer is much more highly organised than the amœba at which we have just been looking. There are here evidently separate and specialised organs. The head is distinguishable from the general mass of the body; the outer covering, which we may call the skin, if you like, is clearly different from the internal portions ; there are two tiny bright spots which are probably organs of vision; while we can clearly detect a small ganglion of nerve substance which fulfils the office of brain. There are also other organs inside the body, all of which have important vital functions to perform.

The first question that a real student of these minute organisms will ask is as to their proper place in the zoological scale, and this is a point about which zoologists are not quite agreed. Professor Huxley ranks them very close to worms, and considers them to be "the permanent forms of echinoderm larvæ;" that is, they agree in many points with an imperfect sea-urchin or star-fish. Mr. Gosse, who has studied these creatures more industriously than perhaps any other man, places them still higher in the animal kingdom, and, while admitting their connection with the lower worms, seems inclined to associate them with insects. The earlier arrangement of Huxley, in which Rotifera are placed as a group of Scolecida, or lower worms, such as inhabit water or are parasitic, is adopted by Nicholson, and is, I think, the safest one to follow at present.

But in whatever way this zoological discussion may be ultimately settled, we have evidently taken a great leap from the amœbean speck of jelly with scarcely any traces of permanent organs to the rotifer with its comparatively high organisation. We have passed through the higher protozoa, such as Polycystins, the more definite modern group of Infusoria (which includes creatures like the familiar paramœcium), the great family of Sponges, the varied forms of Corals, and on to animals like worms. And yet these creatures are invisible to the naked eye, and used to be classed in that *omnium gatherum* once known as the Infusoria. What a wonderful illustration we have here of the rapid advance of modern science, and what a splendid testimony to the value of the microscope as a handmaid to scientific research !

Mr. Gosse prefers to call the gizzard a *mastax*, and contends that it is really a mouth. He says it consists of muscular fibre. Out of it a funnel leads upwards, while a sort of œsophagus runs downwards to the stomach. Inside the mastax are two organs which work like hammers, and supply the place of teeth. They pound down the particles of food on an anvil, and prepare them for digestion. All this is curious to witness, but to see these processes we need higher powers and more elaborate arrangements.

The respiration of rotifers is said to be carried on by means of what is termed a " water-vascular system," consisting of two tubes filled with a watery fluid, from which many shorter tubes proceed into the internal parts of the body. The two longer tubes run into a "contractile bladder," which pulsates like a heart, and so keeps up the circulation.

One curious fact about rotifers must not be omitted, and that is, the sexes are distinct, the females being much more highly organised than the males. The males are more free than the females, but the latter can boast of a superior development, and so probably both are content.

While we are watching the rotifer, it suddenly loosens its hold of the twig to which it was anchored, and swims away, or perhaps tucks in its wheels and crawls in and out amongst the tangled weeds. We can now see that the tail or foot is forked at the end, and slides in and out like a telescope.

There are many varieties of rotifers, but I must not overload my pages with technical words, which would require for their explanation more space than I can now spare. Those who wish to pursue the fascinating subject into details must have recourse to Hudson and Gosse's interesting book, or to the ponderous volume of Pritchard.

I cannot, however, turn away from this group of animals without saying a word about the tube-building rotifers. Perhaps we shall be fortunate enough to find one of these, say the Melicerta.

This creature is a brick-maker and an architect, and can construct as elegant an edifice as one might wish to see. It erects itself upon its telescopic foot and thrusts out above its conical tower, the bricks of which sparkle like so many gems, an expanded

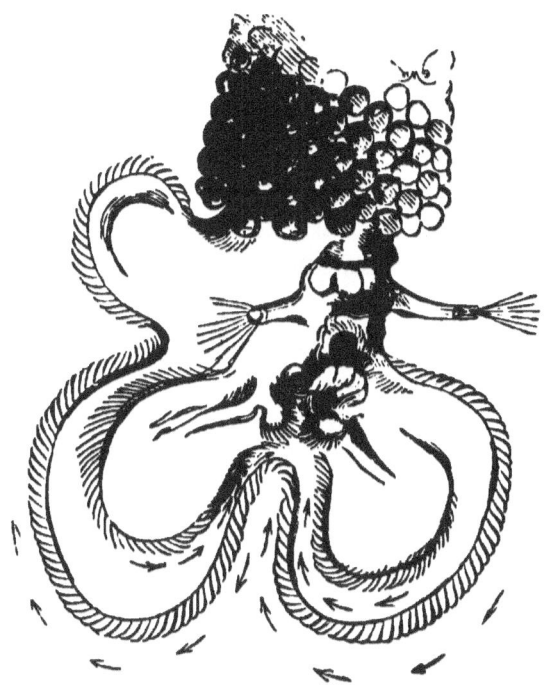

Fig. 30.—*Melicerta ringens.*

head, with four leaf-like structures surrounded with cilia, making, when they are in action, a scene most bewitching to behold. Mr. Gosse was fortunate enough to discover how this tower was made. He observed an organ just above the gizzard which is not always visible, and which he likens to a circular ventilator, and found that this was the mechanism by means of which the tiny mason constructed its bricks. Diverting a stream of minute particles into a kind of mould, the creature cements them together with a sticky secretion, and in doing so changes their appearance, so that they look like glittering pellets; then, bending her head, she deposits the brick into its proper place, and so proceeds from the foundation to the battlements, layer by layer, till the lovely tower is complete.

Professor Williamson tells us that the first layer of pellets is laid, not at the base, but in a ring at about the middle position. "At first new additions are made to both extremities of the enlarging ring; but the jerking constrictions of the animal at length force the caudal end of the cylinder down upon the leaf, to which it becomes securely cemented by the same viscous secretion as causes the little spheres to cohere."

The eye-spots in Melicerta are not usually observed, as they are possessed only in a rudimentary form by the younger ones, and disappear as the creatures grow up.

There is just one other specimen I want to describe before I close this chapter. I have never found this particular species myself, but I have had several opportunities of looking at it in the microscopes of my friends. Any microscopist, however, is almost sure to have at hand a dead specimen mounted on a slip of glass; and even this inanimate object is very beautiful, and by means of diagrams it is easy to describe with sufficient clearness the appearance and the functions of the creature as in life. It is the *Plumatella repens.*

This animal belongs to a group of which there are numerous kinds, and every pond-hunter has met with one or other of them. I am told that in the ponds of Hampstead Heath they are by no means rare. When found in the living state, a number of individuals occur together in a colony. They are polyp-shaped animals, and live together in communities the shape of which is that of a ramifying tube. This tube is dotted at intervals with brown masses of an oval form, from which may be seen in the microscope a number of long pearly tentacles protruding, all decorated along their margins with cilia in constant movement.

FIG. 31.—*Plumatella repens.*

9

These creatures are as much higher in the scale of organisation than rotifers as rotifers are above amœbæ. They are placed by zoologists amongst what are called Polyzoa, a word which means " many animals." Polyzoa constitute the lowest division of Mollusca, so that, in fact, they are poor relations of the snail, the oyster, and the cuttle-fish. They chiefly inhabit salt water, and one of the most familiar of the Polyzoa must have been seen by every visitor to the seaside, though perhaps by the majority regarded as a piece of decaying seaweed. This is the sea-mat, or *Flustra*, which lies about everywhere on the seashore. When looked at with the naked eye, it is exactly like a piece of whitish-brown seaweed. But pick it up and examine it with a pocket lens, and you will see a vast number of lovely crystalline cells, all built up according to the same pattern. If you can dredge up a living specimen, and will place it at once in water, you will see very soon a beautiful sight. Out of these cells will rise multitudes of ciliated tentacles, which wave and rotate in the water in a remarkable way. There is another sea-side polyzoon almost as common as the flustra, and this assumes the form of a miniature fir-tree, for which reason it is called the sea-fir, or *Sertularia*.

There are, however, many fresh-water species of Polyzoa, of which one of the commonest is *Pluma-tella repens*. Let us suppose we are looking at this through the half-inch objective, with the light shining through it from beneath in a somewhat oblique direction, in order not to alarm the timid creatures, and also to enable us to get a better view of the cilia.

We shall first of all see a number of tubes and cells, making together what is called the polypary, or *cœnœcium*, which means a "common house." Then, fixing our attention on one animal, or polypide, as it is termed, we are able to make out œsophagus, stomach, and intestine, the latter bending round and ending in an oval orifice near to the mouth. These are all contained in a bag filled with fluid, and having openings for the mouth and the anus. There is a double system of muscles for the movements of this digestive apparatus. There is a single nervous mass or ganglion on one side of the œsophagus. Around the bag is an investing sheath, from which branch out numerous cells, each occupied by a polypide.

Out of each bag will be seen slowly rising a number of tentacles, which spread out like the rays of a daisy or the feathers of a pheasant's tail. Over the mouth is a kind of tongue or finger-like process, called the epistome, whose office it seems to be to keep out unsuitable atoms of food which the cilia bring within reach. Just at the point where the stomach ends and the intestinal tube curves round may be seen a long, flexible string, called the *funiculus*. This goes to the bottom of the cell, and serves to moor the creature in position. Mr. Slack, in his *Marvels of Pond Life*, to which I am chiefly indebted for the foregoing description, gives us an account of the feeding of Plumatella which he was enabled to observe. He says, " One day a polyzoon caught a large rotifer, which, with several others of its tribe, had been walking over the *cœnœcium*, and

swimming amongst the tentacles, as if unconscious
of danger. All of a sudden it went down the whirl-
pool leading to the mouth, was rolled up by a
process that could not be traced, and, without an
instant's loss of time, was seen shooting down in
rapid descent to the gulf below, where it looked
like a potato-shaped mass, utterly destitute of its
characteristic living form. Having been made into
a bolus, the unhappy rotifer, who never gave the
faintest sign of vitality, was tossed up and down
from the top to the bottom of the stomach, just as
a billiard ball might be thrown from the top to
the bottom of a stocking. This process went on for
hours, the ball gradually diminishing in size, until
at last it was lost in the general brown mass with
which the stomach was filled. The bottom of the
stomach seems well supplied with muscular fibres,
to cause the constrictions by which the work is
chiefly performed; and, by keeping a colony for a
month or two, I had many opportunities of seeing
my Polyzoa at their meals."

The colony goes on enlarging by the development
of fresh cells, but new colonies are originated from
what are called *statoblasts*, germs very much like
the "winter eggs" of some other animals.

The muscles which draw the animal within its
cell are of that peculiar type of muscular structure
called "striped," and which amongst the higher
animals at any rate betokens voluntary action, or the
exercise of will. Has this tiny creature then a will
of its own? Well, it can retract itself into its cell
very rapidly, and this it will do at the least sign of

danger. It also has some kind of feeling, for it possesses at least a rudimentary nervous system. Let it therefore be treated tenderly, and give it plenty of room in the live-box or compressorium; for otherwise, like Melicerta, with its beautiful tube, it may be crushed to death, and suffer who knows how much pain.

X.

A RAMBLE THROUGH CATERHAM VALLEY.

"So fresh, so pure, the woods, the sky, the air,
It seemed a place where angels might repair,
And tune their harps beneath those tranquil shades,
To morning songs, or moonlight serenades."
MONTGOMERY.

ERY few places within twenty miles of London present so many attractions to the geologist as the neighbourhood of Caterham. It was here that the London members of the Wesley Scientific Society enjoyed one of their most successful excursions. And, indeed, it was a real enjoyment. The weather was most propitious—bright, crisp, in short everything that an October afternoon ought to be. We were favoured with the presence of Mr. J. H. Cowham, F.G.S., Science Tutor at the Westminster Training College, who has made this district a special study, and was therefore able to direct us along the most instructive and convenient route, as well as to give us reliable information as we proceeded.

Leaving the River Thames behind us with all its overhanging murkiness, we first of all crossed over a mile or two of Gravel and Alluvium, until at New Cross we met with the London Clay, which extends as far as Croydon. Soon after Croydon was passed, a momentary glimpse was had of the Woolwich and Reading Beds, the lowest members of the Tertiaries. These are made up of sand, pebbles, and clay, and are brought to light in a quarry by the railway side. Then immediately came the chalk, cropping out in all its glory, and forming the most conspicuous geological feature in and around Caterham. The extreme boundaries of the Tertiaries may be observed in many places where the chalk is being quarried—as, for instance, near Caterham Junction ; for on the face of the chalk occur sandy patches or outliers, which are really portions of the Eocene deposits that by the processes of denudation have become almost disconnected, in many cases quite so, from the main masses of the Tertiaries. In times long gone by—how long who shall say ?—the sand and gravel were deposited in crevices in the chalk. Then in process of time, as both sand and chalk were worn down, the thicker portions of the Tertiary deposits in the chalk hollows became separated from the principal part of the same formation, being left as Tertiary islands in a sea of chalk. If then the chalk be quarried at right angles to these sandy courses, their *facies* will seem to be surrounded by the chalk, and so will present the appearance of patches or pipes, as can be seen at Caterham Junction.

This is not the only evidence that the Tertiaries once extended farther south than they do now.

The tops of almost all the hills around Caterham are capped with gravelly outliers of Tertiary age. It is this feature which explains the luxuriance of the vegetation where we should naturally look for the barrenness of a typical chalk district. A boring at Caterham shows that there the Tertiaries have maintained a thickness of eighty-nine feet, notwith- standing the wearing down which has been going on for centuries. As these Tertiary deposits agree with the chalk in general direction, being shaped into the same synclinals and anticlinals, it is clear that they must have been laid before the final upheaval of the chalk took place, for otherwise they would have filled up the hollows caused previously by denudation of the chalk, while the higher portions of the chalk would have been without the gravels that now cap them. Thus is the eye trained by geological methods to read the history of the landscape in the furrows and markings upon its face.

Journeying on in a southerly direction, a number of Secondary formations are encountered. These occur one after the other along the line of route in exactly the same order as that in which they are met with when vertical borings are made into the earth's crust. The Caterham boring already referred to reveals as the order of superposition the Tertiary, the Chalk, the Upper Greensand and Gault, and the Lower Greensand. A boring made in Tottenham Court Road in search of water for Meux' Brewery showed the same order, and was continued into the Oolites.

The most remarkable circumstance in connection

with these strata is that, speaking generally, they
form a hollow basin, in which lie London and its
suburbs, their extremes cropping out in precisely
the same order in a northerly direction from London
as we have stated they do towards the south. The
London Clay which fills the basin stretches from
Croydon to St. Albans ; the chalk from Box Hill
to Dunstable ; the Greensand from Dorking to
Leighton Buzzard ; and the Lower Greensand from
Reigate to Ampthill. The Oolites of the north
thin off as they approach London, and, though they
are met with in the Metropolitan borings, yet they
do not appear in the southern region as do the
Cretaceous deposits.

Next in geological age to the Greensand, forming
part of the Cretaceous series, is the Wealden Clay.
This bed, along with the underlying Hastings Sand,
constitutes the bottom of the Cretaceous formations.
The Wealden Clay resembles the London Clay in
this, that it, also, lies in a basin, the northern and
southern boundaries of which agree in respect to
the order in which the various beds crop out. A
traveller coming from Chichester northwards to
Horsham would meet with the same kinds of deposits
and in the same order as would a traveller going
from London southwards towards Horsham. The
beds both would cross are the Lower Eocene (London
Clay, etc.), Chalk, Upper Greensand, Gault, Lower
Greensand, and Wealden Clay. The advantage
which the Londoner would have over the traveller
from the south is that he would find the various
strata squeezed together more closely in his track,

and consequently he would have less distance to
travel for the same results. In fact, the whole of
these interesting beds may be seen in an afternoon
between Caterham Junction and Tilburstow Hill, a
distance of only some half-dozen miles.

Let us then pursue the walk from Caterham over
the Chalk, leaving the Tertiary outliers behind. In
about half an hour we shall meet with some remarkable Greensand quarries, where the workings
are carried into the hillsides to a distance of several
hundred yards. This Greensand is soft enough to
be easily shaped into blocks in the workings, but
when brought out into the daylight it hardens in
weathering, so as to make durable slabs. Next
comes a flat reach of land extending for nearly a
mile, on which abound the rushes that at once
inform us that we are walking over clay. This is
the Gault, seen to greater advantage in the Warren
at Folkestone, where the most beautiful fossils,
Ammonites, Hamites, Nuculæ, etc., may be picked
up in numbers when the tide is out.

Just as we are entering the romantic village
of Godstone, the Gault gives place to the Lower
Greensand group, which embraces the Folkestone,
Sandgate, and Hythe beds. These latter form the
southern ascent of the London basin ; and when we
have reached the Hythe beds we find ourselves on
a considerable elevation, which is a kind of brink
to another vast basin. It is in this basin that the
Wealden Clay lies, and it stretches away from our
feet over to Hurstpierpoint, twenty-five miles
distant, where again the Hythe Sand is seen, and

after it the various beds we walked over in coming from Caterham, though of course in the reverse order to that in which we then observed them.

Thus much for the physical aspects of the Geology of this district. A few further particulars of a more palæontological character may be added.

The fossils of the London Clay are very numerous in some localities, but not in the one now under survey. Marine creatures, such as Nautilus, crab, fishes, are found, along with estuarine forms, Voluta, Fusus, etc., and sufficiently indicate the nature of the deposit.

The Woolwich and Reading beds consist of mottled clays and sand, and in them are found fossils of both salt-water and fresh-water species. The Thanet beds at Croydon do not appear to be fossiliferous.

Passing on now to the Secondaries, we are at once confronted with the enormous chalk deposits which stretch for a distance of seven miles from Croydon to Caterham, and attaining in some places a thickness of five hundred feet or more. In the quarries and railway cuttings numerous fossils may be obtained with very little labour. Various kinds of sea-urchins (Micrasters, etc.) and ammonites abound. Foraminifera for the microscope may also be got in profusion. These organic remains conclusively show that the hundreds of feet of chalk were slowly deposited by the dropping of the shells of dead animals upon the bed of a vast deep sea, just as is now going on in the Atlantic, from the depths of which the *Challenger* naturalists have dredged up globigerina ooze almost identical in composition with the chalk.

"The dust we tread upon was once alive!"

The Upper Greensand is in some parts a calcareous sandstone, known locally as "Firestone" and "Malm Rock," and is largely quarried for hearth-stones, etc. This will also yield Foraminifera.

The Lower Greensand and Wealden Clay are usually placed together in what is called the Neocomian Series, a subdivision of the larger Cretaceous group. The Folkestone beds consist of clean, light-coloured sands, intersected with ferruginous bands and ribs. They have yielded Exogyra, Terebratula, and other marine shells. In the Wealden Clay is often found the fresh-water mollusc Paludina, while terrestrial plants as well as marine shells also occur, showing that the strata are the remains of an ancient delta. As the deposits have suffered from denudation, the delta must have originally been much larger than the Weald now is, probably covering an area of at least twenty-five thousand square miles, and including the outlets of a river which came down from the north-west, draining a vast territory, of which the British Isles are only a surviving fragment.

These are a few of the points of interest with which this district teems, but far more space than we have at command would be needed to do justice to its varied charms. To find clustered together within the compass of half a dozen miles so many formations is quite exceptional, while the facilities they offer for studying the features of an extensive tract of country without actually having to traverse it are most remarkable. And to all this is added a diversity of lovely. landscape that cannot but be admired, especially by those who can look intelligently upon the scene, deciphering in the gentle undulations and verdant vales, the crumbling sand and overhanging rocks, the fascinating story of Nature's long and unwearied operations, by which she has built up the great hills with the remains of innumerable generations of her offspring, and then has carved and chiselled the material into cliff and valley by the potent agencies at her command, producing by much change and toil the beauty and order that now delight the thoughtful, reverent beholder.

XI.

TINY ROCK-BUILDERS.

"Slime their material, but the slime was turned
   To adamant by their petrific touch;
   Frail were their frames, ephemeral their lives—
   Their masonry imperishable."

MONTGOMERY.

SO much has been written about Corals, from the beautiful though not over-accurate poem of *The Pelican Island* to the more profound volumes of Darwin and Dana, that the amateur geologist is sure to feel a strong desire very early in his pilgrimages to become acquainted with such vestiges of these marvellous rock-builders as are accessible to him. It was amongst the limestones of Wenlock and the Peak of Derbyshire that I was led first of all to cultivate a close acquaintance with these interesting structures; but no account of them would be of much use were I not to refer to other districts and to draw upon the work and writings of others.

For many reasons corals have for the geologist charms that few fossils possess. Their beauty of structure alone, especially when examined under the microscope, would suffice to win general admiration. But their value to the geologist in enabling him to determine ancient physical conditions and the relative ages of the earth's strata is a still stronger inducement to study them. As the coral animal can only fulfil its life functions in water where there are no muddy deposits and which is of a rather warm temperature, the occurrence of fossilised corals in those parts of the earth which are now too cold

FIG. 32.—*Favosites Gothlandica.*

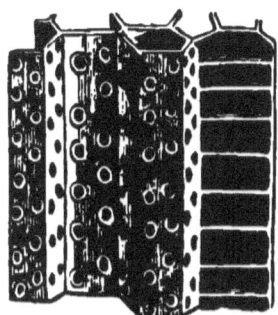

FIG. 33.—Tubes and tabulæ of *F. Gothlandica.*

for their growth indicates vast climatal changes. As to the evidence they present of subsidences and upheavals of ancient ocean beds, to which Mr. Darwin drew special attention in his account of the formation of reefs and atolls, considerable discussion is now going on, and many differences of opinion amongst authorities exist ; but we must not at this point enter into that question.

We will first settle upon what we mean by corals, and determine the place to which they are usually assigned in the zoological scale.

The great sub-kingdom of *Cœlenterata* is divided into Hydrozoa, of which the well-known *Hydra* may be taken as the type ; and Actinozoa, in which corals are arranged. Actinozoa differ from Hydrozoa in the fact that while the body cavity of the latter consists of one tube, that of the former is divided into radial chambers.

Actinozoa consist of the following four orders :

(1) *Zoantharia,* sea-anemones and corals proper ;

(2) *Rugosa,* an indefinite group, made up of extinct fossilised corals ;

(3) *Alcyonaria,* in which are included the familiar dead-man's fingers or *Alcyonium,* the so-called red coral, etc. ;

(4) *Ctenophora,* Venus' girdle, etc.

Until recently corals were classified mainly by means of their hard stony deposits, and were all regarded as belonging to *Zoantharia.* This group was sub-divided into—

(1) *Tabulata,* having horizontal partitions, which split them up into compartments, as illustrated by *Favosites Gothlandica* (Fig. 32, 33), where the polygonal tubes, as well as the tabulæ and perforations connecting the tubes, are shown.

(2) *Rugosa,* having radiating plates or septa in multiples of four, as seen in *Lithostrotion,* an abundant carboniferous coral (Fig. 34).

(3) *Aporosa,* very similar to the last, but having their septa in multiples of six. These did not appear till the Secondary era, and are still abundant. Sometimes madrepores are considered as making up a fourth group called *Perforata.*

FIG. 34.—*Lithostrotion basaltiforme.*

These terms, however, now receive a different interpretation. Professor Moseley thinks most of the *Tabulata* are really Alcyonarians, and Professor Nicholson says that some of the tabulate corals, such as *Millepora,* have been shown to be Hydrozoa; others belong to *Aporosa;* others again, such as Favosites and its allies, belong to *Perforata;* others are referable to the *Alcyonaria;* while

10

others are of uncertain affinities (*Manual of Zoology*, p. 189).

It is clear, therefore, that the term Coral has no definite zoological signification, and that as geologically used it indicates in general most of the organisms now included in *Zoantharia sclerodermata* (*Madrepores*), *Rugosa*, and *Alcyonaria*.

The soft parts of the polype which secretes the hard " corallum" do not differ essentially from the sea-anemone. The stony corals of the geologist were secreted by a colony of such polypes, all of which, however, were united by the common flesh (cœnosarc). The corallum consists of a number of " corallites," or individual skeletons, these having a common calcareous basis.

It is possible to study the habits of the living coral polype, for on our warm southern coasts several species may be met with. If one of the simple corals or madrepores, say a *Caryophyllia* of the Devonshire coast, be placed in an aquarium, it will probably survive. When examined, it will be seen to possess numerous tentacles, in circular sets. The mouth is reddish generally, and has bars of white. The large plates or septa seem to radiate like the spokes of a wheel, dividing the inside basin into chambers. The creature obtains its food by means of cilia which waft the water to the mouth, or by direct capture of its prey with the tentacles. The lime which may form part of the food thus captured goes to construct the " corallite" or skeleton.

The architects of coral rocks are polypes of many

varying species, but they agree in form and structure with the simple polype just described, only they work in colonies, secreting a common stony skeleton. They cannot live at a greater depth in the sea than twenty or thirty fathoms, so that all the vast coral islands and reefs of the Southern seas must have been deposited at that distance from the surface.

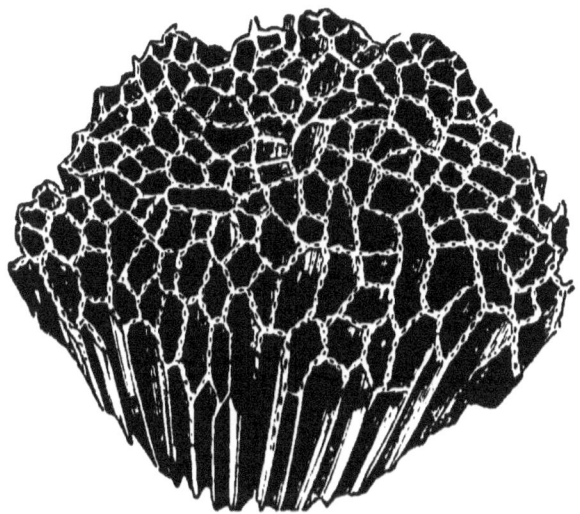

FIG. 35.—*Halysites catenulatus.*

The most important of these organisms are the *Porites*, which construct large rounded masses on the exposed edges of the reef. *Millepora complanata* builds up a honeycomb-shaped structure, the thick vertical plates of which are united at their edges at different angles. On less exposed surfaces the brain coral (*Meandrina*) and the flower-shaped *Caryophylliæ* carry on the work. Dr. Sorby states that the ancient tabulate fossils, so abundant in Silurian and Devonian rocks, are composed of calcite, whereas modern corals are formed of Arragonite, a not very different material, though somewhat differently built up.

Let us now turn our attention to the geological distribution of corals. Their earliest occurrence is in the Silurian rocks, in which *Favosites Gothlandica* (Fig. 32, 33) and *Halysites catenulatus* (Fig. 35) are frequently met with.

Amongst the most ancient and widely distributed of the corals are the *Astræce*, so called from the star-like arrangement of the coral-lites. It is remarkable, too, that this genus is one of the most extensively distributed of the modern corals. *Astræa rotulosa* is abundant in the West Indian seas, while *A. favosa* is as common in the East Indian waters. An illustration is given of *A. ananus* (Fig. 36), a very frequent fossil of the Wenlock limestones of the upper Silurian system. In fact, the whole of Wenlock Edge in Shropshire, as Professor Owen first pointed out, is a Palæozoic coral reef of about thirty miles in length. Here, in the very centre of our land, the haunt of trade and the abode of multitudes, the great sea once rolled and the very dust of the roads was once alive.

In this interesting and picturesque region of

FIG. 36.—*Astræa ananus.*

Wenlock, and more particularly at what is called the Wren's Nest, near Dudley, numerous kinds of corals may be hammered out, among them being *Omphyma, Porites, Heliolites,* the "chain-coral" (*Halysites*), *Cyathophyllum,* and others. When this luxuriance of sub-tropical life is compared with the few species of our warmer Devon and Cornish coasts, the largest of which is *Caryophyllia,* some idea can be formed of the vast changes which our climate must have undergone since those remote epochs when coral islands and coral reefs occupied the site of Britain. In the quarries round about Church Stretton, too, I have found enormous

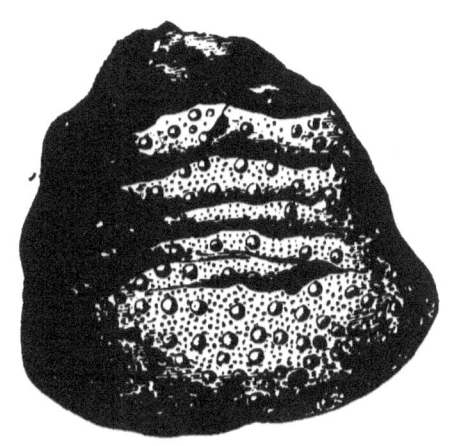

FIG. 37.—*Heliolites interstinctus.*

quantities of corals. In this region, made classic by Sir Roderick Murchison's *Siluria* it is difficult to find a Silurian section without several kinds of coral being seen. The common *Cyathophyllum,* the "petrified ram's horns" of the quarrymen, as well as *Heliolites interstinctus,* which gets into every cabinet of fossils, are abundant. A figure of the latter is given (Fig. 37), and also a magnified portion (Fig. 38), which will illustrate the corallites, or skeletons of the polypes, with the common calcareous basis uniting the corallites together and called "cœnenchyma," thus corresponding to the cœnosarc which joins the soft polypes to one another.

Occasionally a coral deposit will be found in a very friable state, and the fossils will occur as casts or impressions only. The lime which originally belonged to the fossils has been gradually dissolved out by rain-water penetrating into the rocks. Many such casts of *Favosites*, *Cyathophyllum*, etc., may be got near Windermere.

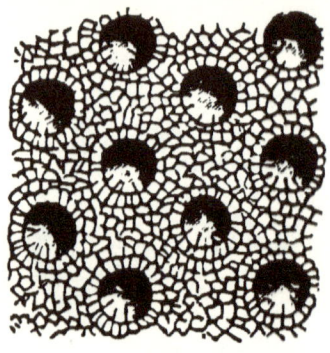

FIG. 38.—Magnified corallites of *H. interstinctus*.

The foregoing remarks will make it abundantly clear that the Silurian period was one of profuse coral development; indeed no fewer than seventy-six species of corals have been described from the Wenlock formation alone.

This applies equally to the Devonian rocks of this country. From these strata fifty-two species of corals have been obtained. The Plymouth limestones are regarded by geologists as portions of an ancient coral-reef which fringed the earlier Cambrian and Silurian rocks. Reef-building corals are abundant in them. It is not always easy to determine which are reef-builders, but there is no doubt as to the *Astræa* (Fig. 36) being amongst them, for they are still at work in many parts of our globe, and these, along with others, are found in the Devonian rocks about Plymouth. Another very common Devonian coral is *Favosites cervicornis* (Fig. 39).

The Devonian corals are difficult to hammer out, as their interstices are filled in with hardened sediment, so that the student will want to cut and polish slices in order to examine their structure and determine their species. Their extreme beauty,

FIG. 39.—Section of *Favosites cervicornis.*

however, will repay the trouble or the cost of procuring polished slabs and microscopical sections.

The climax of coral development was reached in the earlier Carboniferous ages. From the limestones of this system over a hundred and forty species have been catalogued. And yet, as Mr. Etheridge has pointed out, of fifty species from the mid-Devonian rocks none have passed to the Carboniferous, so complete are the distinctions between corals deposited under different conditions. One of the most frequent of the Carboniferous fossils is *Lithostrotion*, a species of which we have chosen as an illustration (Fig. 34). *L. basaltiforme* is a common rugose compound coral. The lighter portion of the figure shows the transverse structure as it appears in microscopical sections. When mountain limestone is weathered, it often looks as though covered with dead twigs. The twig-like prominences are in reality dense masses of corallites, and will very likely turn out to be species of *Lithostrotion*.

The genus *Zaphrentis* is another very common Carboniferous coral, and may be found in a perfect condition weathered out into relief on the limestone walls. *Lonsdalia* looks out from the roadside in many places in Derbyshire, North Wales, and Scotland. It would be impossible and confusing to enumerate even the genera of Carboniferous corals. They occur all through the four thousand feet of the English Mountain limestone, which was probably deposited on the floor of a slowly subsiding sea, and are found in bewildering profusion in the lower Carboniferous strata of Scotland, which seem to have been laid in shallow waters. Besides those already mentioned, it will be easy to obtain *Aspidophyllum*, *Rhodophyllum*, *Clisiophyllum*, from Scotland and elsewhere ; *Cyathaxinia* from the Lake district; the pretty *Phillipsastræa* from Corwen ; and indeed many kinds from every part of Britain where the Carboniferous limestone occurs.

The Permian formation follows the Carboniferous system in geological succession; and as is the case with all other forms of animal life, so with regard to corals, there is an almost complete extinction. So complete is the break in the line of Coral history caused by the Permian cataclysm, that the very nomenclature radically changes.

A good typical specimen of the Liassic corals is the *Isastræa insignis* (Fig. 40). Other genera of the earlier Secondary corals are *Leptophyllia*, *Thamnastræa*, *Thecosmilia*, *Montlivaltia*, etc. At Lyme Regis, Cowbridge in Glamorganshire, near

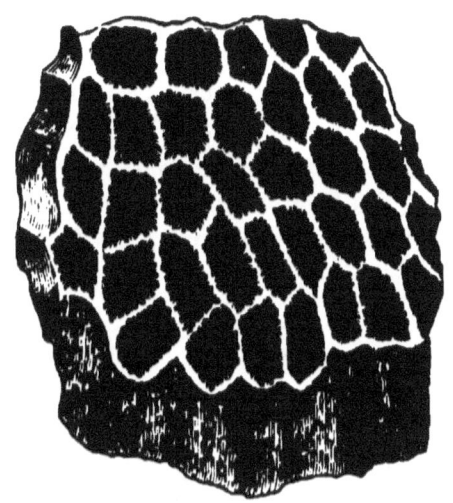

FIG. 40.—*Isastræa insignis* (Lower Lias).

Stratford-on-Avon, and at Marton near Gainsborough, Liassic fossils are plentifully obtained.

Oolitic corals do not differ very much from those of the Lias. *Thamnastræa, Isastræa*, etc., are still abundant, and may be got easily in the quarries near Scarborough. The Coral Rag, whose very name indicates the character of its fossils, is situated nearly at the top of the Middle Oolitic, just above the Oxford Clay. It is not a very thick deposit, reaching only an average of about fifty feet, but it has yielded some fifteen species of fossils. *Thecosmilia*

FIG. 41.—*Thecosmilia annularis.*

annularis (Fig. 41) is a very pretty, large-branching coral of this zone, and is obtained from the Wiltshire beds. Oolitic corals are also plentiful at Malton, in Yorkshire, and near Stroud, where there occurs an ancient "barrier reef" crowded with *Thamnastræa, Isastræa, Thecosmilia,* etc.

The Cretaceous System follows the Oolitic, and is distinguished for the great number of single corals which its various strata contain. As an example of these we present an illustration of *Smilotrichus granulatus* (Fig. 42).

The Tertiaries of Britain afford very few corals. Several kinds are obtained at Bracklesham, in the New Forest, at High Cliff, in the Isle of Wight, and in the London Clay of Sheppey. *Litharæa* (Fig. 43), an Eocene example, is very common.

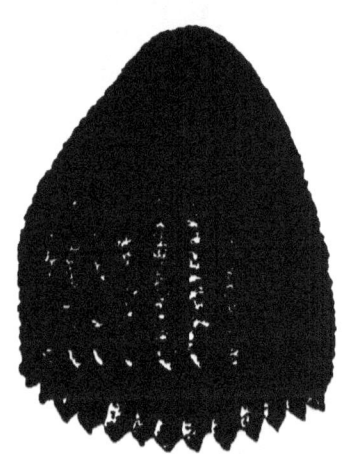

FIG. 42.—*Smilotrichus granulatus.*

This brings us to the close of our review of the geological history of corals, and it now remains only to notice the important part which these organisms have had, and are still playing, in the formation of rocks, reefs, and islands.

Numerous species of polypes contribute to the formation of coral structures. Brainstones (*Meandrina*) form large masses with numerous winding channels; *Astrææ* are studded with holes which are filled with radiating, perpendicular plates ; *Agaricia* have the shape of a mushroom; while numerous others assume the typical shrub-like form. The outside and most exposed portion of a reef is occupied by the genus *Porites*, which build great round-ed masses. *Mille-pora complanata*, of honeycomb appearance, is also able to endure the action of the surf. Deeper down are less hardy species ; while inside are

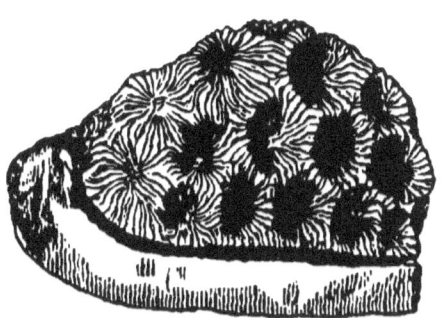

FIG. 43.—*Litharæa.*

quite distinct kinds, such as *Caryophylliæ* and the delicate crimson-coloured *Pocillopora verrucosa.*

It has been doubted whether corals are still continuing their building operations, but it is quite certain that in some localities they are perceptibly modifying the reefs. The action of the sea, the presence of sediment, and the voracity of certain fishes and mollusca explain the apparent inactivity in other places.

A coral island is singularly beautiful. It rarely

rises more than a yard or two above the water, and is richly clothed with vegetation. Here and there rises above the ground a grove of cocoa palms, waving their graceful plumes in the air. The beach is of pearly lustre, and makes a fine contrast against the deep blue of the surrounding water. Before the islet runs a protecting barrier, against which the billows dash themselves and then sink down into the placid lagoon that lies between the barrier and the islet. The lagoon is not completely shut in, but there is a narrow channel between the two ends of the reef and the points of the curved island which they approach. These give entrances to the lagoon for shipping, and also insure a continued supply of fresh water to the haven. That side of the reef which is most exposed to the action of the trade winds attains a greater height than the other or leeward side. This is explained by the fact that on the windward side there is a more abundant food supply for the polypes, and hence their building energy is greater. Some of these reefs are of enormous dimensions. The great reef of Australia is 1,250 miles long, and from ten to ninety miles wide. Dana computes that within the coral region of the Pacific there are nearly three hundred islands, in addition to the reefs that surround other islands, which are of coral formation. When we consider that all these vast accretions are the results of the prolonged and united labours of tiny organisms requiring the microscope for their proper observation, and that the entire materials with which the minute architects carry on their work have been derived from the carbonate of lime which they are continually secreting from the water of the ocean, the mind cannot fail to be filled with astonishment.

> " Millions of millions thus, from age to age,
> With simplest skill, and toil unweariable,
> No moment and no movement unimproved,
> Laid line on line, on terrace terrace spread,
> To swell the heightening, brightening, gradual mound,
> By marvellous structure climbing towards the day—
> Each wrought alone, yet all together wrought ;
> Unconscious, not unworthy, instruments,
> By which a Hand invisible was rearing
> A new creation in the secret deep.
> Omnipotence wrought in them, with them, by them,
> Hence what Omnipotence alone could do
> Worms did."

Formerly it was imagined that these coral structures had been built up from the bed of the sea, and consequently it was predicted that gradually the mighty Pacific would be divided by a vast tropical zone of coral rock, but later on it was ascertained that the polypes cannot live at a greater depth than about twenty to thirty fathoms. Mr. Darwin's well-known treatise on Coral Reefs contains an explanation of the various phenomena concerned which has been universally accepted up to our own day. He supposed that after the polypes commenced to build around the shelving sides of an island at some depth below the surface, the bed of the sea began to subside, the rate of upward growth of the polypes keeping pace with the sinking of the ocean floor. According to this theory, a fringing reef would first be formed rising to within a few fathoms of the

surface of the water. The action of the surf, hurling
up fragments of the rock, shells and various débris,
would do the rest, bringing the reef at length above
the surface and so forming an islet. Inside the reef
there would be a shallow lagoon communicating
here and there with the outside ocean. Thus is
formed the Atoll or true Coral island with its
interior lagoon.

Humboldt has given such a clear and intelligible
outline of Darwin's hypothesis that I cannot do
better than quote it: "An island mountain closely
encircled by a coral reef subsides, while the fringing
reef that had sunk with it is constantly recovering
its level, owing to the tendency of the coral animals
to regain the surface by renewed perpendicular
structures; these constitute, first, a reef encircling
the island at a distance, and subsequently, when the
enclosed island has wholly subsided, an atoll.
According to this view, which regards islands as the
most prominent parts or the culminating points of
the submarine land, the relative position of the
coral islands would disclose to us, what we could
scarcely hope to discover by the sounding-line, viz.
the former configuration and articulation of the land"
(*Views of Nature*, p. 262).

Admirably as this theory fits into the conditions
of the case, it is open to the objection that it
requires many thousands of square miles of ocean
bed to be continually sinking, with consequences
that would naturally be looked for in other places.

Dr. John Murray, of the *Challenger*, has put
forward another explanation. He suggests that

coral growth may have started on a platform of volcanic origin. A volcanic cone may have been worn down to the necessary depth by the action of the waves, or raised to the required height by the continued deposition upon it of the shells and remains of dead marine animals. When the cone, or the base, had acquired the proper depth, the polypes brought to it would begin their operations, building upwards and outwards—the inner portion, or lagoon, being gradually deepened by the solvent action of the sea-water. The advantage of this theory is, that it applies to areas which are being elevated as well as to stationary or subsiding regions ; and there seems to be more evidence of elevation than of subsidence in coral areas. It also explains the curious fact that reefs expand laterally by the more rapid growth on the seaward side, while they remain always only a few hundred yards wide—the inner lagoons becoming larger and deeper as the result of the solvent action of the carbonic acid of the sea-water upon the calcareous elements of the coral structure.

These theories of Darwin and Murray are still being discussed. Not long since, in the *Nineteenth Century*, a formidable attack was made by the Duke of Argyll, not only on Darwin's hypothesis of coral formation, but also on scientific men in general, for what he described as " a great conspiracy " on their part in ignoring Murray and still clinging to Darwin's early explanation. He went so far as to say that, " with all his conscientiousness, with all his caution, with all his powers of observation, Darwin, in this matter, fell into errors as profound as the abysses of the Pacific. All the acclamations with which his theory was received were as the shouts of an ignorant mob. The overthrow of Darwin's speculation is only beginning to be known. It has been whispered for some time. The cherished dogma has been dropping very slowly out of sight. Can it be possible that Darwin was wrong? Reluctantly, almost sulkily, and with a grudging silence, as far as public discussion is concerned, the ugly possibility has been contemplated as too disagreeable to be much talked about. The evidence, old and new, has been weighed, and weighed again, and the obviously inclining balance has been looked at askance many times. But despite all averted looks, I apprehend that it has settled to its place for ever, and Darwin's theory of the coral islands must be relegated to the category of those many hypotheses which have, indeed, helped science for a time, by promoting and provoking further investigation, but which, in themselves, have now finally kicked the beam." He then proceeds to state that corals build on a loose and shifting foundation, which Darwin thought could not be done, that by chemical and oceanic operations the coral structure itself fell to pieces in the rear, and that on this débris the polypes continued to build while they kept up their operations in front, thus gradually raising what would become a reef or a lagoon.

The Duke has probably somewhat exaggerated the reluctance of the scientific world to admit that Darwin was in error, but it is hardly denied by any one that Murray's hypothesis explains some of the coral growths. In this unsettled state we must leave the controversy, with the conviction that the scientific spirit is not likely to do homage long to any theory—however august may be the authority which promulgates it—that does not harmonise with growing knowledge and accumulating facts.

XII.

STAR-GAZING.

" Ye quenchless stars ! so eloquently bright,
Untroubled sentries of the shadowy night,
While half the world is lapp'd in downy dreams,
And round the lattice creep your midnight beams,
How sweet to gaze upon your placid eyes,
In lambent beauty looking from the skies !"

ROBERT MONTGOMERY.

IN the happy, trustful years of childhood how often we looked up with awe at the beautiful stars as they flashed and sparkled " like diamonds in the sky," and thought of them as the homes of angels whither we fain would fly ! We knew those bright orbs better then, perhaps, and loved them more than ever since, for they seemed to bring us near to heaven, and spoke to us of God. But, like many a sweet dream of early days, this vision of a real heaven and an ever-present God has grown sadly dim as the cold mists of rationalism with its pitiless enforcement of bare facts and positive realities have circled round it. Now, alas ! the spirit too often glances into the great lonely sky, and shivers with the horrid fear that because no man knows where heaven is, there may be no heaven at all. O that the heart of the little child might be ever in us ! Then should we not need to go so far away as the stars to seek for heaven, but it would be the nearest thing of all, shining in our very soul, and making it the abode of God.

The stars fulfil many important services for man. We dare not say they were created wholly for his sake, though some of the heavenly luminaries we know were ordained " for signs and for seasons, and for days and years." They may, for all we know, be the abodes of other creatures, or perhaps they are embryo worlds in which are to dwell races of beings high in the scale of existence. But, however this may be, they certainly exert a mighty influence upon human activities and thought.

It is by means of their majestic motions that our chronometers are set, and their transitions and occultations help to make our commerce easy and secure. They light up the path of the benighted traveller with their commingled rays, and chase away his loneliness by inspiring the consciousness that God is near. They appeal to the finer faculties of the human intellect, and supply a thousand fascinating problems for noble thought. Who can describe the undefinable feeling of elevation and content that swells up in the breast when in some blest hour we stand under the calm, silent sky, with all the fever of earthly life and human passion lulled to quiet as if the soul had escaped for a while to heaven ? It is worth something in this distracting world, so full of hardening and roughening experiences, to have the sense of beauty in us aroused now and again by the exquisite variety of form and colour which the starry heavens display. Life is felt to be better worth having for the power to enjoy the wondrous spectacle of the starlit sky, flecked with the ever-changing cloudlets that fly before the moon, and glittering with the silvery beams of Sirius and Vega, the orange hues of Capella and Procyon, and the lustrous tints of Arcturus. And when one of those rarer phenomena which sometimes glorify our firmament is witnessed, and the comet's spectral train sweeps into vision, or the meteoric shower passes with rain of gold before our eyes, then what depths of awe and joy are opened within us !

But beyond all this the stars exercise a moral and spiritual ministry for us, and help to bring us to a bliss that commerce and wealth, intellectual culture and æsthetic refinement, of themselves fail to secure. The contemplation of their glories draws the devout mind into closer sympathy with God ; and, notwithstanding the sobering effect of exact knowledge of Nature's wonders, tends to make us heavenly-minded. It was a pleasing fancy of the ancients that the stars in their courses emitted mystic harmonies, and even in this unpoetical age it may be said by those who are quick to hear their Maker's praise :

> " There's not the smallest orb which thou behold'st
> But in his motion like an angel sings
> Still quiring to the young-eyed cherubim."

I. The first thing the stars have to say to those who have ears to hear is, that *there is a Creator :* " The heavens declare the glory of God, and the firmament showeth His handywork."

La Place scoured the sky with his telescope, and told his age that he found no God there ; but what the wise men of this world have often failed to discover because they were blinded by the dust of Materialism, babes and sucklings, simple and un-learned, have distinctly seen. Many a child who knows not what the stars may be, and many a devout man to whom astronomy is a sealed book, has gazed with rapture on those bright gems that make the brow of night resplendent, and has felt, with a strength of conviction that no mere argumen-tation could beget, and that no gloomy rationalism could destroy, that there must be a great Being some-where Who made these shining orbs. Napoleon I. once heard a knot of officers stating some objections to the belief in a Creator, and at once, with that common sense for which he was far more remarkable than for his piety, he silenced them by the blunt remark : " It's all very well, gentlemen, but who made the stars ? " Atheism is still without an answer to that question. It traces them back to the primeval fire-mist, and assumes certain physical forces in virtue of which they have become what they are, but the difficulty is only evaded. Whence came that fire-mist, and how were originated those laws ? Who made the stars ?

O ! it is sad to see so many looking around with professed intelligence upon all the marvels of

Nature, and finding nothing but a " fortuitous con-
course of atoms," or the " survival of the fittest "
out of an indeterminate number of possible worlds ;
while they imagine that they are establishing their
superiority of intellect when pouring contempt on
the venerable belief that " the Lord by wisdom
hath founded the earth ; by understanding hath He
established the heavens." What though you cannot
find Him, does that demonstrate that He does not
exist ?   Have you been everywhere in search of
Him ? Have you taken "the wings of the morning "
and scoured infinite space ?   Have you descended
into the lower parts of the earth and explored all
her glittering mines ?   Have you soared into the
sky and questioned all the stars ?   In some far-off
region whither you cannot go, He may sit enthroned
in light.   In some subtle form which you, with
glimmering intelligence and imperfect instruments,
are unable to detect, He may exist.   Neither in
the ponderous masses that cross the field of your
telescope, nor in the tiny specks that you place
under your microscope, may you expect to behold
any ethereal essence which may be called God ; but
yet there are such traces of vast power and wisdom
in all directions, in the minutest diatom or protozoon
as well as in the most stupendous starry constella-
tion, that only the obstinately prejudiced or the
incredibly foolish can go on repeating : " There is
no God."

Our faith may be treated with polished scorn, our
opinions may be called narrow or benighted, our
arguments may be regarded as weak and limping ;

we may be told again and again that we are not
abreast with the times and with modern thought;
yet do we deem ourselves wiser and happier than
our critics, in seeing God everywhere and discerning
the activities of an Infinite Mind in all the lovely
and wondrous things that Nature discloses before
us. For this God is our Father and our Friend.
He loves and guards His children, and helps us in
our toils and trials. He is a Comforter, soothing
us in our griefs and sorrows. He is a Saviour,
plucking us out of the grasp of sin and Satan. He
gives peace to our troubled conscience, and rest to
our wearied, tempted soul. He supports us through
all the rough pilgrimage of life, and will uphold us
in the trying hour of death. And so the convictions
of the devout heart harmonise with the teaching of
the gentle stars, which, though voiceless, yet are, in
their own way,—

> "For ever singing, as they shine:
>   'The Hand that made us is Divine.'"

II. Not only does the contemplation of the starry
heavens confirm our belief in the existence of the
Creator, but *it tends also to exalt our conceptions of
His Sovereignty.*

Consider the vastness of God's domain, and how
it displays the majesty of Him Who sustains and
governs it. Even to those who are accustomed to
astronomical measurements, it is bewildering to
contemplate the extent of the universe, and the
magnitude and velocity of the myriad worlds of
which it is composed. Language, and even imagi-

nation, are miserably inadequate to - express the grandeur and massiveness of the heavenly host, or the amplitude of those remote firmaments which are only dimly seen with the highest telescopic powers.

The great globe on which we live has not been fully explored, and yet it is only a speck of dust amid the crowds of worlds that coruscate in the lustrous concave of the sky. The bulk of Saturn is a thousand times that of the earth, while the mighty Jupiter is fifteen hundred times as large as our planet. But the sun himself is five hundred times as great as all his satellites put together, and is equal in cubic measurement to a million and a quarter of such globes as ours.

When we turn our attention from the magnitude of the planets to the dimensions of their orbits, we are utterly incapable of grasping the stupendous distances that confront us. A locomotive which would travel round the earth in a month would require over two thousand years to traverse its orbit, and the incredible space of sixty thousand years would be necessary in order to accomplish the journey round the orbit of Neptune.

But these measurements even, although far beyond the scope of our faculties, dwindle into nothing when compared with the extent of the innumerable worlds that shine like glittering specks upon

"That broad and ample road
Whose dust is gold and pavement stars."

Our sun is in reality one of the fixed stars, and

is the nearest of them. His next neighbour, *Alpha Centauri*, is twenty millions of millions of miles away ; while of the few which are near enough to permit of their distances being calculated, some are so far from us that their light, which darts along at the rate of over one hundred and eighty thousand miles in a second, requires fifty thousand years to reach our earth. Of these remote worlds some are known to be several thousand times larger than our sun, and so numerous are they that twenty millions of them are made visible by the telescope, while there are besides vast clusters of systems too distant to be separated into distinct points of light.

> " Awake, my soul,
> And meditate the wonder ! Countless suns
> Blaze round thee, leading forth their countless worlds !
> Worlds in whose bosoms living things rejoice
> And drink the bliss of being from the Fount
> Of all-pervading Love. What mind can know,
> What tongue can utter all their multitudes ? "

How great is He Who metes out these heavens with the span, and fills with His presence and His power this illimitable realm ! O that our thoughts of Him could be as great !

Some, however, in meditating upon the vastness of God's domain have feared that man might seem so insignificant to Him as to be beneath the reach of His love and care, and they have repeated with tremulous doubt the old soliloquy : " When I consider Thy heavens, the work of Thy fingers, the moon and the stars, which Thou hast ordained ; what is man, that Thou art mind-

ful of him ? and the son of man, that Thou visitest
him ? "

But nothing that God has made can be unworthy
of His regard. Great and small are relative terms,
and derive their meaning mainly from man's imperfection. We are awed by bigness. The sight of
a surging crowd thrills us, and we travel over
continents to gaze upon a mountain. But we
must not think that our vulgar emotions have
any counterpart in the character of God. Everything is of importance to Him that affects the
welfare of His creatures. We degrade God by
supposing that the busy multitudes of mankind
that inhabit our earth in successive generations
are of no more account to Him than clouds of
dust sweeping through the air, or swarms of
ephemeræ dancing for the short hour of their life
over the dark pool which, in the same day, is both
their cradle and their grave. Our poor standards
of greatness are not used in heaven.

When once we have learned to regard God as
our Father, we shall not be tempted to think that
He can look down upon our woes and disasters
through stony eyes and with heart unmoved.
Even the dim reflection of His Fatherhood which
we see in our family relationships teaches us that
to a parent nothing can be of greater interest than
the happiness of the child. The smallest detail
of food or dress is thought worthy of attention.
Caresses and endearing words would be valueless
to a child if it were allowed to go unfed. But
is there any love of earthly parent so unselfish

or so wise as the goodness of our Heavenly Father manifested in the arrangements of Nature and emphasized in the revealed Word? How, then, should He remain content and cynical, absorbed in the contemplation of His own perfections and the adoration of angels, while countless myriads of His offspring are weltering in tears and anguish, ready to perish for lack of the light and strength which He alone can impart?

Besides, it may be that the redemption of our race is an element in the happiness of other beings, and is necessary to the moral equilibrium of all worlds. Let but one star slip from its orbit and every other will eventually be affected. So man's apostasy is perhaps related to other disturbances in God's realm in such a way as to make his salvation an essential factor of universal holiness and bliss.

But however this may be, the earth is a portion of the Creator's dominions, and it is not incredible that He should desire it to be governed by His laws. Kings and nations concentrate all their energies upon winning back provinces that have rebelled, or that have been wrested from them. A few years ago I witnessed a touching spectacle in Paris, when she was still suffering from the wounds of the German conquest. Close by the spot where the palace of her last emperor used to rear its majestic façade, stands the statue of Strasbourg, more dear to France than ever now that the city of which it is the emblem is lost. Around the neck and arms of that sculptured figure

are hung wreaths and immortelles, and upon a
set day each year thousands of Frenchmen in its
presence utter vows of undying remembrance and
love.   Shall kings and people cherish the memory
of their lost territories, and the King of kings take
calmly the spoliation of His domains by enemies
whose bad ambition would impel them, Titan-like,
to wage war upon God?   Infinite as is the greatness of the Deity, He is glorified by His solicitude
for man's happiness ; and lowly as man may be,
he has a soul which, under the inspiration begotten
by the consciousness of God's love, may rise to
angel-like perfections.

III. Another fact to which the starry heavens
bear emphatic witness is *the unity of the Author of
Creation.*

It is to the Scriptures that we must go for clear
and final declarations that the universe is the work
of one infinitely wise and powerful Being, but many
striking confirmations of this doctrine are furnished
by astronomical phenomena.   To whatever part of
the stellar region the attention is directed, there is
discovered, amid great diversity of detail, a complete
uniformity of plan, evidencing the presence and
supremacy of one intelligent Will.   Just as Columbus
opened out a new world in which the laws of nature
were identical with those of the old world, so the
discovery of one planet after another, one star after
another, has but furnished illustrations of what
applies also to our earth.   It was a thrilling
moment for Galileo when through his newly constructed telescope he gazed for the first time upon

the satellites of Jupiter, and found in that far-off region the same kind of movements as those which he affirmed, in spite of persecution, were characteristic of our planet. And ever since that day, astronomy has continued to produce fresh evidences of the uniformity of nature and the oneness of nature's Original. The silvery Venus, showing by her phases that she passes through transitions like those of the moon ; the ruddy Mars, reflecting from his polar snows the light which upon the same principles glorifies our sky ; the mighty Jupiter, belted with fleecy clouds that tell of atmospheric influences like those with which we are familiar ; the many-ringed Saturn, testifying of forces which operate all through our world ; and the remote Uranus, trembling in its orbit in obedience to gravitation, and so leading to the discovery of its remoter neighbour Neptune, —all these are held in their places by the same conditions as those which rule the earth. And in the depths of space are detected by means of the magical spectroscope the identical elements which compose our globe, and the laws of light and colour which determine the hues of our many-tinted flowers. The Father's house has " many mansions," but they all stand in some essential relation to each other and bear the impress of one presiding Intelligence.

The most remarkable instance, perhaps, of uniformity of law is the revolution of the heavenly bodies round others greater than themselves. This, like many another discovery of modern science, is seen to be referred to in the Scriptures, now that a better understanding of nature has supplied the

key with which to unlock the meaning of the sacred
language. In all parts of the sky are binary, triple,
multiple stars, vast systems and constellations kept
in unchanging association with each other by the
same forces that govern the falling mote. " The
bands of Orion," which awoke the wonder of the
patriarch Job, present the precise aspect now that
they did when he beheld them ; still hanging like
a triplet of diamonds upon the belt of the giant who
gropes along the track of the sun. These distant
worlds which, by reason of their remoteness, seem
to be but stationary points of light, are in reality
journeying rhythmically around some invisible centre,
so far away that from the Creation till now only a
minute arc of the vast circle has been traversed. It
used to be thought that this phenomenon was referred to in the question in Job : " Canst thou bind
the sweet influences of Pleiades ? " The Chaldean
word used here is *Chimah*, which means a pivot, or
axle, and it was affirmed by astronomers that
Alcyone, the brightest star of the group, was the
actual spot upon which the heavens were hinged as
they swept round in a stupendous orbit requiring
for its completion over eighteen millions of years.
This is now known to be not quite correct, but
there is a far-off centre towards which our solar
system is approaching. What is that centre ? we
may ask. Is it the City of Light, whose Founder
is the living God ? Do some faint rays shine upon
our dull eyes from that glorious throne which is
more brilliant than a thousand suns ? And do we
need only an instrument subtle and powerful enough

in order to behold "the saints' abode"? This we
may never obtain, but we have spiritual vision
which penetrates far beyond the reach of the most
elaborate telescope, and enables us to realise something of heaven's holy light. "Faith is the substance
of (the giving substance to) things hoped for."

This uniformity of Nature, which is here taken as
showing that 'the Lord our God is one Lord,' is
sometimes spoken of as being nothing more than
the persistence or unchangeableness of Law. But
what is law without a Lawgiver? "What do we
mean," asks Paley, "by the Law of Nature, or by
any law? Effects are produced by power, not by
laws. A law cannot execute itself. A law refers
us to an agent." Uniformity of law, then, demon-
strates the existence of a single supreme Mind in
Nature. "The Lord He is God ; there is none else
beside Him."

The great danger attending this false interpretation of the uniformity of Nature is that it begets
gloomy and erroneous views concerning the character
of God. We ought not to suppose that the Creator
has no power to mould or suspend or overrule by
higher laws those ordinary methods of His procedure
which we call the Laws of Nature. These fixed
principles of the Divine government are arranged in
the interests of God's creatures, and they encourage
foresight and prudence, the highest of the virtues ;
but to say that the Deity will never interfere with
them is simply to make one of those sweeping and
unwarrantable inferences which are the bane of
much that goes by the name of philosophy.

There are, of course, laws which, like their Author, are immutable, and it is for the good of the whole universe that these laws should never fail. But even here there is room for the Divine tenderness to show itself in giving us help in our feeble endeavours to live in harmony with what is true and right. It is this feature in God's character which touches most deeply the universal heart of mankind, and awakens in us the holiest aspirations. In one of the principal cathedrals of Europe I witnessed a simple act which thrilled me as many a more illustrious deed would have failed to do. Vast crowds of people had thronged to the temple to take part in one of the chief religious festivals of the year, and through the multitude a prince of the Catholic Church, followed by a long line of dignitaries all magnificently arrayed, walked in solemn procession. But not even the gorgeous vestments of the ecclesiastics, or the swelling cadences of the organ and choristers which reverberated through the edifice, had such an effect upon the congregation as was produced when the stately cardinal paused for a moment on his march, and stroked the hair of a chubby-faced child that knelt close by upon his father's knee. Every eye moistened as it beheld that gracious act, the most beautiful and natural thing in the whole service. And yet what condescension of man's can be so great as that of God, " Who became poor, that we through His poverty might be rich," and Who still dwells with the " humble and contrite," that He may destroy within their souls all that is discordant with His holy law ? And is He not ever the same, like His bright, unchanging stars ? Then, my soul, fix thine unfaltering gaze upon Him as thou dost seek release from all thy sins and griefs that fetter thee, and like the trembling fugitive from the house of bondage, who never paused while he could gild his face with the beams of the blessed star which hung over the land of liberty, thou shalt find emancipation from the galling tyranny of sin, and shalt dwell for ever in the abode of truth and righteousness. Thou shalt rise above the stars, for thou art greater than they, and God thy Strength and Saviour shall shine in thy sight with a glory that shall surpass thy sweetest visions upon earth.

12

XIII.

AN EVENING AT THE MICROSCOPE.

"The very meanest things are made.supreme
With innate ecstasy. No grain of sand
But moves a bright and million-peopled land,
And hath its Edens and its Eves, I deem."

L. BLANCHARD.

OCCASIONALLY I am honoured with a visit from some of my friends who come to see whatever microscopical wonders I may chance to have. In a small aquarium I endeavour to keep a few, at least, of the tiny plants and animalculæ which I have managed to fish out of the ponds and ditches and brooks of the neighbourhood. Tangled water-weeds, floating scum, prolific duckweed, dripping bog-moss, bedraggled reeds and rushes, anything and everything that could be hauled out and squeezed into my jars, have been promiscuously collected, and, after a cursory examination and rough clearing, tossed into this miniature world which is bounded on all four sides by glass, and covered at the bottom with pebbles, loam, and,water-plants. Sometimes, no doubt, my friends feel bored with my prolix descriptions of the tiny creatures exhibited, but not seldom I am rewarded by observing an enthusiasm that answers to my own, as some more than ordinarily lovely organism has been brought up by the pipette from that not very attractive-looking aquarium.

I want to describe in a simple, non-technical way a few of the more familiar objects obtained in this way. I shall have but little to say to those who are accustomed to work of this kind, for I wish to write now exclusively for younger and comparatively inexperienced disciples of the microscope. I am continually hearing it affirmed that writers on scientific subjects never seem to think that students of nature must begin at the beginning, and that by plunging all at once into the intricacies and technicalities of zoology they usually repel the inquirer and lead him to the conviction that all natural science consists of nothing but dry facts and unpronounceable names. There is, perhaps, some truth in such remarks, but on the other hand it should be borne in mind that while it may be well to try to make the alphabet of knowledge attractive, yet the marvels of nature can be fully appreciated by those only who are willing to take some trouble to study them accurately and systematically.

Let us now take a dip into the aquarium and see what will come up. Selecting a minute portion of the jungle-like mass of water-weeds, I place it in a small glass trough or in the live-box. Having fixed the one-inch objective in position, I lay the trough on the stage of the microscope and proceed to focus

the lens. In a moment or two all is in readiness
for the inspection of my visitors. And what a
spectacle it is which they gaze upon ! It will not
be long before all sorts of ejaculations and expressions of amazement and delight will be uttered.
All round the field, and interlacing every part of it,
are microscopic water-weeds, while clinging to what
look like thick stems and silvery twigs, or darting
about through the microscopic jungle, are weird and
wondrous creatures which rivet the attention of the
observer. In these few drops of water in which to
the naked eye there seemed to be almost nothing,
there is now seen to exist a crowded population.
There is the exquisitely beautiful Bell-animalcule
(*Vorticella*), the elaborately organised Rotifer or
Wheel-animalcule, the Hydra, hanging on to the
white root-fibre of the duckweed (*Lemna*) with its
tentacles spreading out like a tuft of branches, the
whole not very dissimilar in appearance to a miniature palm-tree, while, here and there, flitting about
with extraordinary velocity, may be caught a glimpse
of the slipper-shaped *Paramœcium*, the pink-eyed
Euglena, or the restless water-flea, which keeps up
its incessant evolutions like an untiring acrobat.

But all these wonders cannot be fully described
in the comparatively short space of time that my
friends can give me at one visit. I proceed, therefore, to single out two or three of the objects seen,
and separate them as far as possible from the
rest.

We will first of all look at the minute vegetable
organisms contained in the selected drop of water.

The one-inch objective has given us a magnification of about fifty, but now let us turn the nosepiece round and bring the quarter-inch lens into position. This is a glass constructed by the eminent opticians, Messrs. Powell & Lealand, and it will give a magnification of over three hundred linear with ⎯the B eyepiece of Ross.

The first of these microscopic plants to which I shall draw attention is a Desmid. Here is one, of which an illustration is given (Fig. 44), called *Closterium.* It is a familiar object, but in this case

F<small>IG</small>. 44.—*Closterium striolatum.*

familiarity does not breed contempt. Being of a bright green colour and full of chlorophyll, which requires the action of sunlight, it follows that the proper time for collecting desmids is during summer and autumn, and they are generally found near the surface of the water, where the sun can get at them. These pretty little plants lie almost at the very bottom of the botanical scale. They belong to the natural order *Algæ*, of which seaweeds are the best known types. But they are one-celled Algæ and as individuals are invisible to the naked eye. They are exclusively fresh-water organisms, and are never found in the sea. In this they differ from their

allies the Diatoms, which thrive in both fresh and
salt water. My experience leads me to the conclusion that they are most easily found in shallow
ponds on open moors and on damp bog-moss. If a
bit of this bog-moss (*Sphagnum*) feels slimy to the
touch, the probability is that we have come upon a
crop of desmids. When found it is as well to wash
them into a glass bottle filled with clean water,
where they will soon settle on the sides and bottom,
from which they should be detached by a camel's-
hair brush, and deposited on a slip of glass for
inspection. Most desmids are free cells, but in
some cases several individuals are grouped together
in the form of a star or disc; others, again, take the
form of long threads or ribbons, and are consequently
called filamentous desmids.

Desmids possess a transparent membranous
envelope or case, entirely destitute of silica, the
flinty material which accompanies diatoms. This
case contains the chlorophyll, or green colouring
matter, which renders these tiny plants so conspicuous. They, no doubt, constitute the chief
food of fresh-water animalculæ, and almost every
observer of them has seen the rotifer greedily suck
out the contents of the envelope and cast away the
empty, but still beautiful, case. While living they
have the power of gliding through the water with
an even graceful motion, while their hyaline covering, sparkling with emerald points, and filled with
diamond-like granules, helps to make up a vision
of beauty surpassing that which Aladdin's lamp
revealed.

What gives to the plant this power of independent movement? Does it possess tiny hairs, or cilia, with which it lashes the water or rows itself along, or is the cause to be found in the generation and ex-halation of oxygen? Here is a question which I have to confess I am unable to answer, although I have peered at these fairy-like organisms with prolonged and tireless curiosity through almost the best optical apparatus that science can supply, and I could wish my readers no better fortune than that they might hit upon this well-guarded secret of Nature. For those who possess good appliances I would suggest this problem for their study. The desmid should be carefully observed on a dark background, with and without a condenser, in a natural condition, and also stained with aniline dyes. But these are details into which I have promised not to enter now.

It is not difficult to cultivate desmids. They should be kept in a watch-glass filled with their own native water, and covered over with a plate of glass to keep out dust and prevent too rapid evaporation. If absolutely necessary to renew the water, a little rain-water should be added. There are two methods by which desmids reproduce themselves. The first is by cell-division or fission. The clear space in the centre of the desmid may be seen gradually en-larging, without, however, the fracture of the membrane. In the course of two or three hours the two halves are separated, each commencing to grow and continuing till the parent form is reached. Another method of production is that called conjugation. Two individuals approach each other, and at length mingle their contents together, after which a circular body makes its appearance, called a *Sporangium*, that is, a spore-vessel. Ultimately a cloud of spores is poured out, and from them a multitude of desmids ultimately develop.

Unfortunately, no medium has yet been discovered in which these lovely objects can be preserved as mounts, so as to retain their colour. Hantzsch, of Dresden, has got as near to this desirable end as any one, but complete success has never been attained. He used a mixture of pure alcohol, distilled water, and glycerine, which, being nearly of the same specific gravity as water, retards the contraction of the cell. I have had several specimens in my cabinet for some years which have not appreciably altered. But even this method of mounting does not meet the difficulty of providing a perfectly air-tight cell, which is, of course, absolutely indispensable to the prevention of evaporation for an indefinite period.

Another object now claims our attention, and is one that will richly repay careful inspection. This is the ever-beautiful Volvox, familiar enough, but enshrining deep mysteries that even the restless eagerness of nineteenth-century science has not solved. This is an object well worthy of being sought after, and fortunately it can be obtained at almost any time in the year. It is, however, somewhat fickle in its attachments, for in localities where it has been found repeatedly, it will at another time be sought in vain, although there is apparently no reason for its disappearance.

Now look at it through this half-inch objective. Did you ever see anything more lovely? Watch that gracefully rolling sphere as it slowly revolves on its axis across the field of view; notice its delicate tracery forming the boundary lines of six-sided cells; observe the profusion of pear-shaped dots from whose apices are projected those very

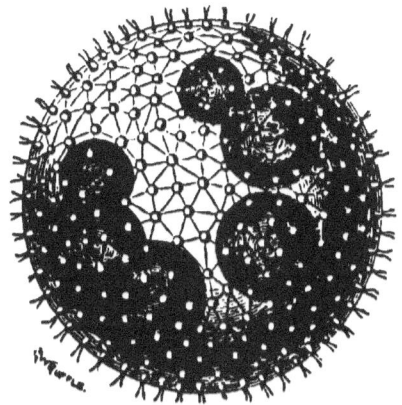

Fig. 45.— *Volvox globator.*

fine gossamer-like hairs, or cilia, which penetrate right through the outer envelope, and with swift movement row the volvox along, and tell me whether even Nature's casket contains any gems more won-drously fair. Within the globe are smaller globes. With a higher magnification these are seen to be growing volvoces, and not infrequently there may be found within these a third generation, all carrying on their marvellous gyrations within the parent cell. After a while the mother, or the grandmother,

will grow weary with age and cease her activities—
she will lose her fresh greenness and perish, and the
young, panting for liberty, will break through her
ruptured sides, and escape into the tiny water-world
where they were born.

Under still higher powers and with the help of
a weak staining agent such as iodine and diluted
sulphuric acid, it will be seen that the green spots
are united by extremely fine protoplasmic threads
which pass through the sides of the hexagonal
cells. There may also be detected minute atoms of
colourless protoplasm, which is probably the agent
of cell-division. When the cell is ripe it opens
without abruptness, as if there were a natural vent
which is gradually prepared for this crisis, and the
ensphered young glide out. At first they are tied
to the parent by long filaments which prevent
revolution, but soon the threads give way and the
sweets of perfect liberty are tasted. Whether there
is actual revolution of the young within the parent
globe, or whether the apparent revolution is due
to an optical illusion caused by the motion of the
mother-cell, is a point on which authorities differ, and
is one about which I am not prepared to pronounce
dogmatically.

There is, however, another reproductive process
which may be witnessed in the later part of the year.
Two distinct kinds of cells are developed within
some of the larger globes, the one an egg-sphere
(*Oosphere*), and the other a sperm-sphere (*Anthero-
zoid*). In higher plants these correspond to pollen
and ovules. The egg-spheres are fertilised by the

antherozoids, and a kind of spore is the result. These escape from the decaying parent and lie dormant till their vitalities are quickened by re-

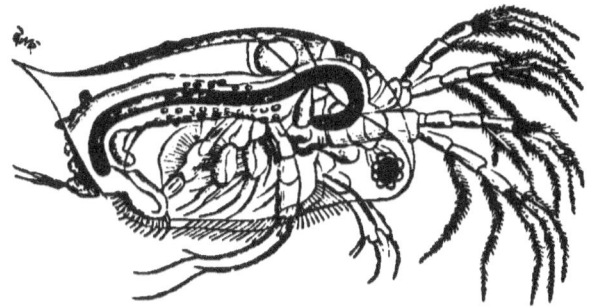

FIG. 46.—*Daphnia pulex* (Male).

turning spring, when they will at once start upon their new career and develop into perfect volvoces endowed with the powers essential to cell-division.

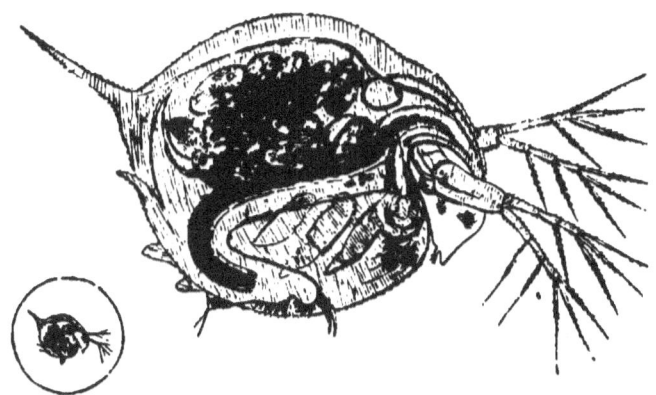

FIG· 47.—*Daphnia pulex* (Female).   Natural size and magnified.

Now we must leave this fascinating object, though much more might be said, and look at one or two of those other curious organisms that lie about or move with slow and laborious efforts or else with quick and jerky movements within the microscopic field.

There is an object which for a long time has seemed to be inviting attention by frisking across the field, and sometimes remaining for a moment within vision: what can it be? If fleas lived in water, one might jump to the hasty conclusion that it really was a young flea. Its antics are certainly quite as fantastic as those of the "lively flea." This, no doubt, explains why it is called the water-flea. We must not, however, be misled by names. These tiny creatures are very different from the ordinary flea, as may be seen by looking at both objects under a low power through the microscope. The flea is an insect proper, with rudimentary wings, and breathes the air like other insects. But if you closely observe this nimble dweller in the water, you will see that it has delicate appendages to the head, like branched antlers. Moreover, its body is soon perceived to be encased in an almost transparent shell, having two valves, and its feet are prolonged into plates, very much like the gill-plates of fishes, only, of course, very minute.

Water-fleas belong to a group of animals called *Entomostracans*, which form a sub-division of Crustaceans, so that they are really related to shrimps and lobsters. They are very ancient animals, and can be traced back at least to Carboniferous times, and seem to have been as numerous in the standing pools of those vast forests which produced our coal, as they are now. The covering, or carapace, of these lowly Crustaceans is very similar in nature to the substance called *chitine,* which composes the outer portions of insects. The head of *Daphnia* is not covered by the shell, and the creature has but one eye—a bright, inquisitive-looking organ it is, too, and apparently quite capable of doing duty for two. There are very few males compared with the vast number of the females. The contractile organ whose working can easily be seen, acts as a kind of heart, and there are five pairs of legs. The female produces two kinds of eggs. The " summer eggs," from ten to fifty in number, are deposited in an open space between the valves of the carapace, and are kept there till the young are ready to be hatched ; but the " winter eggs," which are only two in number, are placed in what is called the saddle, on the back of the carapace, where they remain till hatched by the returning warmth of spring.

The evening is wearing on, and we must not permit ourselves any further diversion in watching this frolicsome creature, for there is still another tiny animal that I am anxious to prepare for the inspection of my visitors, whose presence I had already detected in a cursory and preliminary examination of the material with my pocket lens. This is the *Hydra.* On one of the long white fibrils—or roots as they may be called, only they hang free in the water—of the duckweed in the aquarium I observed a specimen of this most interesting group of animals. To those accustomed to its appearance, it can be detected even with the naked eye, for it measures at least an eighth of an inch, quite a respectable size compared with the creatures we have already been looking at. We must treat this animal with great care, lest in arranging it for the microscope we should despoil it of all its beauty. At first it looks like a mere speck of greenish jelly. But wait a moment, and you will see it protrude its tentacles from the lengthening body and throw them out like the graceful leaves that surmount the beautiful palm.

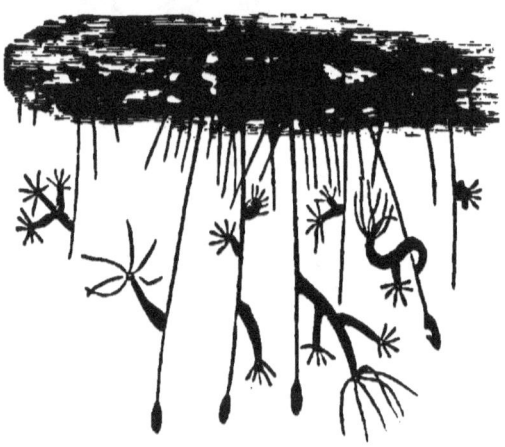

Fig. 48.—*Hydra viridis.*

We must just say a word or two respecting the place which this wonderful creature occupies in the animal kingdom, for nothing is more interesting or instructive to the student of zoology than to find out the similarities or affinities between the various creatures that he is trying to understand.

The Hydra is one of the so-called fresh-water polypes—which really means a many-footed animal. Properly speaking, it applies only to corals, but is usually made to refer also to other *Cœlenterata* or hollow-bodied creatures. At the bottom of this great class stand the *Hydroid Zoophytes,* of which the hydra is the typical example. It consists of a tubular or cylindrical body, which expands into

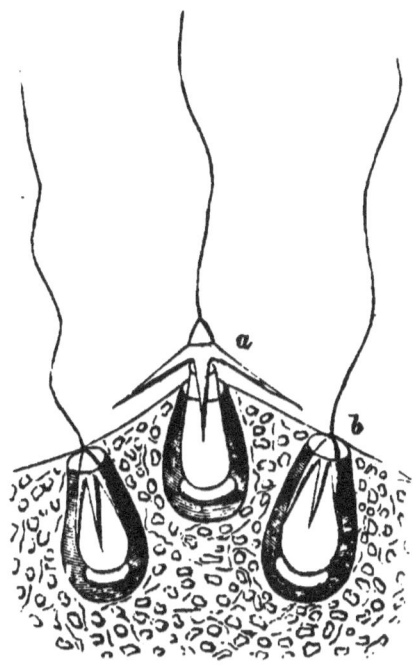

FIG. 49.—*Stings of Hydra.*

tentacles surrounding the mouth, its other end terminating in an adherent disc or foot. The tentacles are capable of great extension, and are used as organs of prehension. The hydra has an extraordinary power of multiplying, for even when divided by any injury into a number of pieces, each portion will develop into a perfect polypite. The usual method of reproduction, however, is by budding, an example of which is seen on the left of our illustration (Fig. 48), and also by means of eggs which are deposited in winter.

Perhaps the most curious fact about the hydra is, that it possesses certain arrow-headed stings, by means of which it is able to benumb such minute organisms as it wishes to capture for food.

These stinging threads may be got for examination by cutting off one of the tentacles, and looking at it through an objective of one-sixth or one-eighth focal length, giving a magnification of, say, three to four hundred diameters. Then let the light pass through it obliquely, and there will be seen all around the edge a number of small cells or capsules, from which a very fine thread will be emitted. These stinging organs are similar to those possessed by sea-anemones; and bathers have occasionally been made aware of the fact that the Medusa jelly-fish has the same kind of weapons.

The hydra is remarkably simple in structure and in organisation. The whole body is composed of similar substance called sarcode, in which is enclosed a colouring matter. Every part has a high contractility, and though the creature is eyeless it is very sensitive to light, as the microscopist soon discovers. The outer portion of the sarcode is probably a trifle denser and harder than the inner, and hence the two words ectoderm and endoderm are used to denote the two integumentary layers.

The hydra being done with, it was time to stop

our pleasant occupation, though many other objects
quite as beautiful and instructive might have been
fished up out of the water and weeds that I had
brought home. Indeed, even while we were actually
engaged in looking at the specimens specially singled
out for study, there were other creatures lying or
crawling about, or occasionally flitting across the
field of vision. Minute algæ or water-weeds, spores
and embryos, the flower-like vorticella, eel-like
worms wriggling about in the water, and glistening
as though made of silver, the frustules of dead
diatoms, and I know not what besides : for a few
drops of pond-water and a small fragment of star-
weed, or duckweed, constitute a thickly populated
world. None of our crowded cities are so filled
with life as these tiny water-worlds through which
the enraptured microscopist delights to travel.
There they are born or are germinated, there they
develop, there they spend their fairy-like life,
there they perform the useful offices of cleansing
away all manner of impurities, or, like creatures far
higher than themselves in the scale of organisation,
supply food for animals even more useful·than
themselves. Thus are we taught by such studies
that in Nature nothing is insignificant, nothing without its uses and its beauties of form and structure.
And in regard to all these minute organisms nothing
impresses the mind more deeply than the beautiful
adaptation of all their parts to the conditions of
their existence. Whatever their place in the animal
series, whatever the nature of their environment,
they have evidently been so conditioned by a

13

Being possessed of perfect knowledge and infinite benevolence.

" The minutest throb
That through their frame diffuses
The slightest, faintest motion
Is fixed and indispensable
As the majestic laws
That rule yon rolling orbs."

XIV.

TRILOBITE HUNTING.

" You may trace him oft
By scars which his activity has left
Beside our roads and pathways— .
He who with pocket-hammer smites the edge
Of every luckless rock or stone that stands
Before his sight by weather stains disguised,
Or crusted o'er with vegetation thin,
Nature's first growth, detaching by the stroke
A chip or splinter, to resolve his doubts."

WORDSWORTH.

O geologist is ever likely to forget his
first trilobite " find." Amongst my fossil
treasures—too rarely visited, alas !—
there lies a fragment of one of these
curious crustaceans which, imperfect as it is, possesses
a charm for me that many far more elegant and
valuable objects lack, for it takes me back to a
sunny holiday in Shropshire when, amid most
beautiful natural surroundings, and in company of
enthusiastic friends, I enjoyed my first real trilobite
hunt. I have been to more prolific grounds since
then, and have knocked out more perfect specimens,
but not one of them has dislodged from its supreme

place in my regard that crumpled eyeless *Trinucleus*
of the Salopian bank of Caradoc
shale.

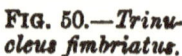

Nowhere are trilobites more abundant in this country than in the
well-known Wenlock limestone near
Dudley, although it is not easy to
chip out a perfect specimen. Here
are found the *Calymene Blumenbachii*,

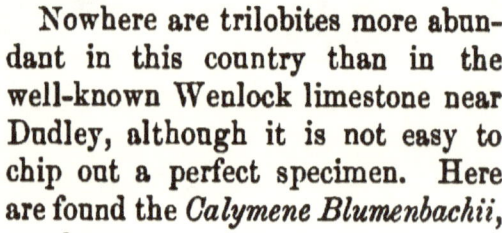

FIG. 50.—*Trinu-
cleus fimbriatus.*
so long
known as
the "Dudley locust," the
Phacops caudatus
(Fig. 16), and scores of
other species. But there
are many other places
where numerous species
have been obtained. The
Menevian beds of St.
David's have yielded
large quantities of tri-
lobites, amongst them
being the magnificent
Paradoxides, which is
sometimes a couple of feet
in length. In the more
northerly districts of
Wales, as, for example,
at Port Madoc, these
fossils are abundant,
and the *Olenus* literally

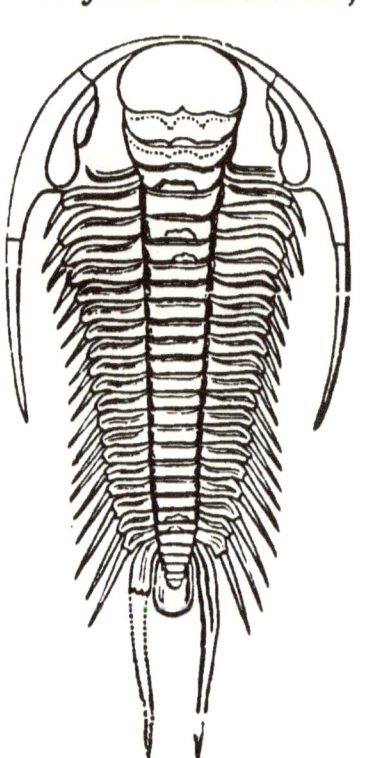

FIG. 51.—*Paradoxides Tessini.*

crowds the lower Lingula flags at Maentrog. The

whole of this district is classic ground for the geologist. Exquisite scenery affords additional attractions to the delights which the Knight of the Hammer never fails to experience when pursuing his favourite hobby. All along through the wild, weird valleys, and over the rugged mountains, there are ever-changing and most fascinating panoramas. When Dolgelly is reached it will be found as good a centre for the trilobite hunter as for the tourist who is in search of bewitching scenery. In this neighbourhood may easily be obtained the *Concoryphe*

Fig. 52.
Agnostus pisiformis
(Upper side).

Fig. 53.
Agnostus pisiformis
(Lower side).

and the *Agnostus* (Figs. 52, 53), which, as we shall see, is of great importance for the light it sheds on the subject of the development of the trilobite, while the Llandeilo flags of the locality never fail to yield the pretty *Ogygia*. The Silurians near Llangollen contain numbers of *Phacops, Calymene, etc.*, and here, too, the most enchanting landscapes are spread out in all directions. It is one of the charms of geology that its practical study brings us into the presence of natural beauties which the average tourist never discovers, while at the same time it adds to these attractions of scenery a loveliness which only appears to those who perceive the hidden meaning that lies beneath the surface of Nature's works.

Silurian trilobites occur in large numbers also near Hereford, where *Phacops*, *Homalonotus*, and other genera may be found.

The Devonian strata furnish trilobites, but not in anything like the profusion that characterises the Cambrian and Silurian beds. Dr. Taylor refers to Newton Abbot as being a good hunting-ground for them, but I was not fortunate enough to obtain any when I visited that romantic district.

The carboniferous limestone of the Derbyshire Peak is pretty sure to reward the searcher after trilobites. At Castleton I met with *Phillipsia*, which along with *Griffithsides* is frequently to be obtained from the shales and belts of limestone in that locality. These are of great interest as presenting the last scions of a noble race which in earlier geological times enjoyed a sort of supremacy over the less richly endowed, though in some respects more highly developed, Molluscan fauna.

In geological range, as just intimated, the trilobites are confined to the Primary rocks. They were exceedingly prolific in the Cambrian seas, having reached almost their zenith of size and development in early Cambrian times ; rapid variation proceeded during the Silurian age, while distinct degradation marked the Devonian history of these creatures ; and in the next period, the Carboniferous, they became rare and small, ultimately passing out of existence altogether before the advent of that transitional age of confusion and catastrophe which closed the Primary epoch and prepared the way for the Secondary. Hence, whenever a specimen of the easily identified trilobite is met with we may at once feel certain that the bed in which it occurs is older than the Permian or the Coal.

There is perhaps no chapter in the volume of Creation more complete in itself, or less related to other chapters, than this which gives us the history of the trilobite. Page by page as we turn from one tablet to another of Nature's great Stone-book we see old organisms becoming extinct and new ones gradually taking their place, all witnessing to the continued existence of creative energy. Coming in along with the very oldest of terrestrial creatures—for it is not demonstrated that *Eozoon* of pre-Cambrian times is organic—this remarkable animal goes through its cycle of existence, from the eyeless *Agnostus* on to the huge *Paradoxides* by a rapidity of development almost startling—for both belong to the earlier Cambrian deposits—and then on through long centuries of slow variation and deterioration to the comparatively insignificant Carboniferous genera which were unable to hold their own in the fierce struggle for existence with the mighty Vertebrates that were by this time taking possession of both land and sea. Whence they came, from what root-stock they sprouted, and whither they went, into what surviving forms they transmitted their expiring energies, can be conjectured, but not conclusively determined.

Scientific classification is based on the nature,

structure, and affinities of the objects concerned. For a long time naturalists were quite undecided as to the precise position which on these grounds ought to be accorded to the trilobite, owing to the fact that they knew next to nothing concerning its structure. It seemed so utterly different from every creature now known, and furnished so little of suggestion in its necessarily defective fossilised form that it was only recently that anything like a final and authoritative opinion was arrived at as to its true position in the animal kingdom. The very names of the more familiar genera show how ready the earlier naturalists were to confess their ignorance in regard to these singular fossils. *Calymene*, the hidden, *Agnostus*, the unknown, *Asaphus*, the uncertain, *Paradoxides, etc.*, all reflect the attitude of mind of those who were first called upon to deal with these perplexing creatures. As to their general Crustacean characters there has been but little doubt since the time of Brongniart, and their partial resemblance to the *Isopoda* (or wood-lice) as well as to *Limulus* (or king-crab) is now definitely agreed upon. Even a superficial comparison between the fossil king-crab shown at Fig. 57 and a typical trilobite will demonstrate the accuracy of this conclusion, and when we come to compare the larval forms of the two creatures this will be made still more clear. In Haeckel's *Systematic Survey* trilobites are placed amongst the *Branchiopoda* or "gill-footed" crustaceans, and so are regarded by him as relatives of the water-fleas. But as no traces of breathing organs, either aquatic or aerial, nor any vestiges of feet have been observed, that arrangement, to say the least, is

FIG. 54.--Under side of King-Crab (*Limulus*).

somewhat unsatisfactory. Some kind of breathing

organs the trilobite of course possessed, and Dr. Henry Woodward believes he has found traces of legs ; but these are matters of so indefinite a character that they are not sufficient for the purposes of scientific classification, and, as our readers will be aware, the very term " gill-footed " is unfortunate. Moreover, the highly organised compound eyes of the trilobite demand that it should be placed much higher in the Crustacean scale than that in which the lowly water-fleas are ranged. Nicholson puts it in an order by itself a little lower than the *Merostomata* (king-crab, etc.), and both are regarded by him as lower than the *Isopoda* (wood-lice). Here for the present it remains, although, if the structures met with in some recent American specimens should turn out to be legs, which Dr. Woodward thinks really are so, but which others regard as only calcic arches, it would probably be necessary to place it in some other position.

A very large number of species of trilobites have been made. It would be as well if many of them could be unmade, a process which happily seems very probable. Darwin has written an account of the *Origin of Species*, but who shall give the history of the Manufacture of Species ? Geology, of all the natural sciences, has suffered most from this needless and confusing multiplication of species· This, of course, has partly arisen from the fact that when only fragments of a creature were obtained it was not always possible to determine its characters, and yet it was necessary to give it a name ; but the evil has been aggravated in consequence of the eager-

ness to name fossils which has been displayed by
many geologists, some of whom were but poor naturalists. Now and then, from no better ambition, we fear,
than to perpetuate the name of the finder, and still
oftener from his ignorance of zoology, new genera
and species have been made, to the utter bewilder-
ment of those who now set out to study the
particular creature concerned. Differences of the
most insignificant kind, such as would hardly be
sufficient to constitute a variety, and some of which
were certainly not permanent, have been taken as
sufficient reason for the starting of a new species.
Owen has pointed out that the trifling differences
between *Asaphus caudatus* and *Asaphus longi-
caudatus*, chiefly in respect of the tail-spines, may
only mean that the one is male and the other
female. Then again, so much evidence has of late
been procured to show that trilobites, like other
Crustaceans, moult and go through various stages
of metamorphosis, that very likely a considerable
number of so-called genera and species are really
nothing more than different links in the life-chain
of the same individual. Who knows whether the
lowly, eyeless *Agnostus* may not after all be only,
as Owen hints, "the larval form of some large
trilobite"? When we come to deal with the detailed
structure of the trilobite, we shall be confronted
with many other suggestions of this sort. Mean-
while we still have fifty genera and four hundred
species of trilobites, awaiting, we hope, some diminution, as fresh knowledge is obtained concerning
their embryology and life-history.

The structural details of trilobites furnish a means whereby palæontologists are enabled to arrange the numerous species in well-defined groups or families.

The *Agnostidæ* are eyeless and small, having not more than two body-rings, the shields of the head and tail being nearly equal. (Figs. 52, 53.)

The *Olenidæ* or *Paradoxidæ* are characterised by their long bodies, which are divided into many segments. The tail-shield is small, and curved spines are often found along the sides. (Fig. 51.)

The *Asaphidæ* are mostly made up of large oval-shaped trilobites, having about eight body-rings, and being covered with a smooth carapace.

The *Trinucleidæ*, containing some of the prettiest of trilobites, have the head-shield large, with a long process or spine hanging from each side of it. (Fig. 50.)

The *Cheiruridæ* consist of seven genera. The number of segments is eleven, and they are free at their ends.

The *Calymenidæ* have rough carapaces, and the body usually contains thirteen segments or rings.

Another family called *Phacopidæ* had large facetted eyes and eleven body-rings. (Fig. 16.)

The *Lichades*, consisting of only one genus, have small heads and a tail with a broad limb.

The *Prætidæ* are interesting as embracing the last of the trilobites, the Carboniferous *Phillipsia* and *Griffithsides*. Although these are of small size, the number of the body-rings is usually nine. The carapace or body-covering of *Phillipsia* is generally rough or granulated, and seems to have

contained more living matter than was the case
with the others. (Fig. 55.)

The *Acidaspidæ* have from eight to ten body-
segments, the sides of which (pleuræ) are turned
backwards.

There are also the *Bronteidæ* with large expanded pygidium or tail, the *Harpeidæ* with
horseshoe-like head-shield and numerously seg-
mented body, and lastly, the *Cyphaspidæ* the
head-shield of which is prolonged
into spines.

It is from the structure of the
trilobites, moreover, that it has
been found possible to determine
the conditions of their existence
and their general habits.

The chemical composition of the
carapace affords a sufficiently accurate indication of the character
of the habitat of the creature; as,
for instance, the living and granulated covering of *Phillipsia*, just
referred to as living in the carboniferous seas. In

FIG. 55. — Head-
shield and Tail-
shield of *Phil-
lipsia.*

other cases the carapace seems to have been more
chitinous, like the wing-cases of insects.

The fact that the body-covering is so often found
in separate portions makes it certain that trilobites,
like crabs, underwent the periodical process of
moulting. The head-piece or cephalic shield is
generally found alone, the thorax or ringed part
often so, and the pygidium also frequently occurs
separately. The moultings of *Phillipsia* are always

found in two parts, the head by itself and the body and tail joined together. (Fig. 55.) In the case of *Calymene* the ringed thorax is often met with by itself, while not unfrequently the rings are separated from one another.

The mouth of trilobites, by the simplicity of its structure and the absence of antennæ, warrants the inference that these creatures were "bottom-feeders," that is, they fed from the ground. Mr. Salter, who made trilobites his special study, arrived at the opinion that they lived in the mud and even found their food in the organisms which it contained, very much after the manner in which the earthworm derives its nutriment from the soil. They could, however, swim, and probably were not averse to making a meal off any dainty mollusc that might come in their way.

No traces of legs have been found, save those very indefinite structures already referred to, but it is supposed that they had fleshy or cartilaginous feet, like the footstalk of the *Lingula,* and which of course has left no fossilised remains. It is certain too that some species could coil themselves up like the wood-louse ; others, as the *Homalonotus,* were probably not able thus to protect themselves against their foes.

But the most remarkable feature in the morphology of the trilobite was the eye (Fig. 56) ; this varies with the species. In *Homalonotus* it is small and protuberant like that of the lobster. The eye of the *Bumastus Barriensis,* a common fossil of the Woolhope beds, 'eems to have been protected with a strong lid. In many species, the eye is compound, like that of the house-fly or dragon-fly. As already observed, some trilobites were eyeless, these being generally the simplest in structure, such as the *Agnostus*. They are, however, found in company with more highly developed forms.

The compound eyes of the trilobites in their fossilised condition present the appearance of a crescentic ridge, on which the numerous facets, in some cases as many as four hundred, are geometrically arranged (Fig. 56). Dr. Buckland

FIG. 56.—Compound eye of Trilobite (*Asaphus caudatus*) and Ocelli of ditto magnified.

described these ridges as being "like a circular bastion, ranging nearly round three-fourths of a circle, each commanding so much of the horizon that when the distinct vision of one eye ceased that of the other began." Their particular form and position he regarded as "peculiarly adapted to the uses of an animal destined to live at the bottom of the water; to look downwards was as much impossible as it was unnecessary for a creature living at the bottom; but for horizontal vision in every direction the contrivance is complete."

It follows then that the environment of the

trilobite, so far as physical conditions are concerned, did not greatly differ from what we now see in nature. These primeval seas and the atmosphere above them acted as media of light, just as water and air now do. The *Limulus* or King-crab has compound eyes that bear the same relationship to light as did those of the trilobite, and the same optical laws were evidently in operation. To quote again from Dr. Buckland's *Bridgewater Treatise,* " The earliest marine animals were furnished with instruments of vision in which the minute optical adaptations were the same that impart the perception of light to crustaceans now living at the bottom of the sea. . . . With regard to the atmosphere, we infer that had it differed materially from its actual condition, it might have so far affected the rays of light that a corresponding difference from the eyes of existing crustaceans would have been found in the organs on which the impressions of such rays were then received. Regarding light itself also, we learn from the resemblance of these most ancient organizations to existing eyes, that the mutual relations of light to the eye, and of the eye to the light, were the same at the time when crustaceans endowed with the faculty of vision were first placed at the bottom of the primeval seas, as at the present moment."

Having dealt with the geological distribution of trilobites and their structure and classification, it now only remains to consider the question of their descent.

Whatever may be thought of the evolution theory as an explanation of the mode of creation, the efforts to substantiate that theory have certainly proved fruitful in bringing to light many homologies of structure in the vegetable and animal world that had previously been overlooked. There are, it is true, many respected students of Nature who fail to see in homologous structures an invincible argument in favour of community of origin, and who therefore regard evolution as unproved, but who nevertheless accept it provisionally or as a valuable working hypothesis.

In any inquiry bearing on the origin of an animal form, Geology of course must be heard. But in regard to the ancestry of the trilobite Geology is singularly deficient in supplying suggestions. When trilobites had already reached their zenith there were but a few phyllopod crustaceans in existence, and these were far removed from the trilobite in structure, while no contemporaneous mollusc throws the least light on the subject. Darwin says (*Origin of Species*, p. 286) : " It cannot be doubted that all the Cambrian and Silurian trilobites are descended from some one crustacean which must have lived long before the Cambrian age." If the evolution theory be true, this of course is so ; but it ought to be pointed out that an *ipse dixit* of this sort is entirely destitute of argumentative value. It is an admission that palæontological records fail to reveal the ancestry of the trilobite. Barrande, than whom no one can speak with greater authority on trilobites, went so far as to say that their evolution was " un produit de l'imagination, sans aucun fondement dans la réalité."

14

The imperfection of the geological record may be pleaded as an excuse for the absence of transitional forms, but then, as Prof. St. George Mivart says, "it *is* an excuse." When we reflect that the trilobite was built up after an entirely different pattern from any older or contemporaneous creature whose fossil remains have come down to us, that it had essentially different nervous, digestive, and circulatory systems, and that it possessed highly complex eyes and other organs of sense, it is certainly very extraordinary that there should be no geological record of transitional forms of even the minutest character to enable us to trace the descent of this curious animal or to discover its generic alliances with any previously existing creatures. Sir J. W. Dawson does not exaggerate when he observes in reference to trilobites that "nothing short of a very large faith in the imperfection of the geological record can suffice to account for their evolution." (*Chain of Life*, p. 80.)

When we turn to the consideration of the after history of the trilobite, we find that both Geology and Biology afford a little help in discovering structural relationships with other crustaceans. As to the value of these similarities and affinities in evolutionist speculations different readers will probably entertain different opinions.

I have already pointed out the striking resemblance which *Belinurus*, a fossil king-crab from the coal measures, bears to a typical trilobite (Fig. 57). It was during this geological period that trilobites became extinct, and it is interesting to find a king-crab of the same age so much like them. King-crabs are very peculiar creatures, and seem to be connected with other crustaceans in only a remote sort of way.

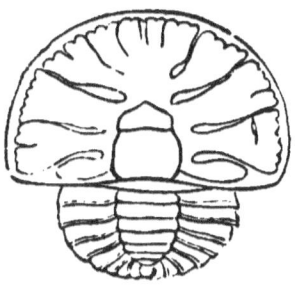

FIG. 57.—Fossil King-Crab (*Belinurus trilobitioides*).

FIG. 58.—*Prestwichia.*

Before leaving the egg, the embryo acquires all its main features, and at that early stage shows a remarkable resemblance to the *Prestwichia* (Fig. 58),

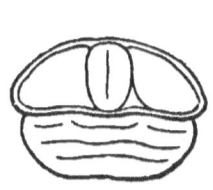

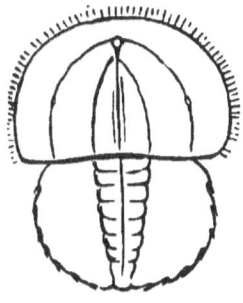

FIG. 59.

Larva of recent King-Crab.

FIG. 60.—Larva of Trilobite.

a trilobite found in the " Penny-stone nodules " of Shropshire. This resemblance may be seen by comparing the larva of a recent king-crab with a larval trilobite (Figs. 59, 60). A reference to Figs.

54, 57, 58, 59, and 60, will show that the resemblance is maintained through succeeding stages up to the adult condition.

Crustacean metamorphosis has of late years been a most fascinating study for many naturalists. Just as we have the *pupa* and *chrysalis* of insects, so we have various stages in the development of crustaceans, and many members of this class are strikingly alike in their early condition. There is the *Nauplius* stage, a term derived from the name of one of the lowliest crustaceans, the *Zoëa* or water-flea stage, the *Mysis* or opossum-shrimp stage, and others. The lobster passes through half-a-dozen of these stages, and the trilobite, according to Barrande, who enjoyed exceptional opportunities for studying it, passed through even more, resembling in its earliest stage the *Ostracoda* in having no joints to the body. Not that all crustaceans pass through every one of these metamorphic stages, but some go through one and some through another, and thus their place in the zoological tree is determined.

It is upon these principles that a line of descent has been drawn, which connects the trilobite with the king-crab. The *Belinurus*, one of the ancient king-crabs, appeared at about the geological time when trilobites were dying out, as has just been observed, while the young of the *Limulus*, the king-crab of our day, is similar to the adult trilobite; hence it has come to be a widely received opinion that *Limulus* has the best right to be considered the descendant and representative of the ancient and noble race of trilobites.

There is another creature which has a distinct likeness to some of the lowlier trilobites ; this is the *Bopyrus* (Figs. 61, 62),'a parasite of the shrimp. As it is probable that all parasites are degraded forms, it is regarded by some as not at all unlikely that one branch of the older crustacean class, possibly a section of the trilobite group, has found its present resting-place in this diminutive parasitica creature. The illustrations are of the female, which

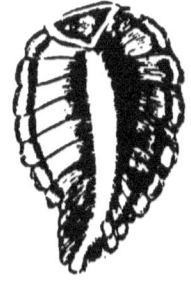

FIG. 61.—Shrimp Parasite
(*Bopyrus crangorum*)
Upper side.

FIG. 62.—Shrimp Parasite
(*Bopyrus crangorum*)
Lower side.

seems to be more degraded than the male, having lost its eyes altogether, while the male preserves them in a rudimentary condition. This has perhaps arisen from the different habits of life which belong to the female, and it is instructive to observe that it is this more degraded form which most nearly approaches the trilobite in appearance.

Dean Buckland and others have regarded the *Serolis* (Fig. 63) as being very closely related to the trilobite. Certainly this creature has an old-world look about it, and presents a remarkable similarity of form to that of the typical trilobite of the Cambrian age. The principal trilobites of this geological period were characterised in general by having the thorax divided into a larger number of segments than is the case with those of later ages, while the tail portion is not so well developed, and the side lobes are profusely fringed, as may be seen in *Paradoxides* (Fig. 51). The *Serolis*, which is a crustacean isopod plentifully occurring in the seas around Tierra del Fuego, possesses all these features, and, in addition, has compound sessile eyes arranged in crescentic lobes, just as many trilobites have, while it also resembles the Silurian *Phacops caudatus* (Fig. 16) in having a movable tail-shield. There are differences of structure in regard to the mouth organs and antennæ, but these are fragile appendages, and would not easily be preserved as fossils, even if trilobites possessed them, which it is thought was the case with some species.

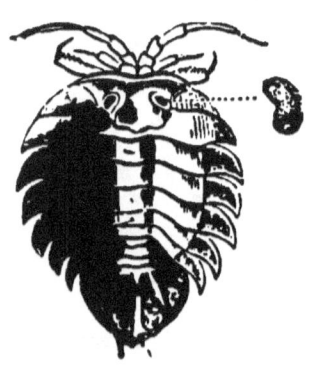

FIG. 63.—*Serolis Fabricii*, with eye magnified.

The *Apus productus*, a common denizen of our ponds, has also been suggested as being related to some species of trilobite. The *Apus* in passing through the *Nauplius* stage takes on a trilobite appearance, and when it is fully developed, its sixty pairs of legs cannot but remind us of the marginal fringes which adorn so many of the older trilobites

These many slight resemblances to other animals, whatever they may suggest as to descent and modification, do certainly show how large a portion of the crustacean area was occupied by trilobites all through the vast ages of palæozoic time. From the king-crab to the shrimp-parasite is a long distance, and yet trilobites by their varied functions and organs evidently stretched out over that distance; and though nothing absolutely conclusive can be inferred in regard either to the origin or the descent of the trilobite, yet these numerous affinities afford a field extensive enough for the speculations of the most imaginative and the inquiries of the most industrious.

XV.

WHAT IS CREATION?

" Through knowledge we behould the World's creation,
How in his cradle first he fostred was,
And judge of Nature's cunning operation,
How things she forméd of a formless mass."

SPENSER.

" Creation is great and cannot be understood."

CARLYLE.

THERE have been at different times and still are many theories of Creation. The word "theory" is very ambiguous. It is necessary, therefore, to lay down what we mean by it. Amongst the older philosophers it denoted speculation. It is now very frequently used in opposition to "practice," as signifying the principles or doctrines underlying and determining art. In scientific discussions it is often taken as equivalent to "hypothesis," that is, a suggestion, or even inference, for which, it is admitted, there is not sufficient evidence, but which, on account of its agreement with a greater or less number of circumstances, we are led to adopt provisionally as a law or an explanation of a certain series of facts. This is the sense in which we shall use the term, as it corresponds accurately enough with its ordinary signification in modern philosophy and science.

It is obvious that in inquiries which are concerned in the discovery of natural law, it is highly serviceable, nay, absolutely necessary, to generalise or to make inferences of a more or less sweeping character for the purpose of giving definiteness and directness to further observations or experiments. Faraday speaks of the hosts of such deductions that he was continually fashioning and slaying in his magnificent researches. The value of a theory framed thus will of course be determined by the number of facts that it harmonises. A mere figment of the imagination may serve to guide observation, but it will not, ordinarily, be so fruitful in results as the hypothesis which is suggested by some fact or phenomenon that it seems to explain. Occasionally a happy guess may turn out to have hit upon a universal law, but that will be a very remarkable exception. The old saying that "Nature abhors a vacuum" gives no reason why water rises in the pump. But the theory that the phenomenon results from the pressure of the atmosphere upon the water outside the piston or sucker of the pump is so closely allied with many other similar phenomena, such as the rise and fall of the mercury in the thermometer and barometer, and the changes in the level of the mercury as the instrument is carried up a mountain, that no one now thinks of disputing the accuracy of this explanation.

John Stuart Mill made it the chief aim of his

logical writings to show the insufficiency of the Baconian method of collecting facts and drawing from them conclusions of a continually widening scope. These empirical laws, as the inductions of the Baconian method are called, will usually be safe and accurate, but they may also be barren.

In the search for Nature's laws, we must sometimes go before her complete revelations, though we must allow her to point the way. Bacon's doctrine was the heroic remedy for the venerable tyranny of Aristotle and the Schoolmen, but the true method of scientific discovery lies between the Aristotelian deduction and the Baconian induction. All theories, however, must be based upon ascertained facts, and must be verified by comparison with other related facts, before they can be considered as worthy of confidence. Newton's emission theory of light was seen to be inconsistent with the fact that atoms, however infinitesimal, could not be projected from vast distances upon the delicate structures of the eye without injuring them. Young's undulatory theory, although emanating from a far more obscure source, was found to harmonize so completely with all such phenomena as reflection, refraction, and colour, that it quickly drove Newton's hypothesis from the field.

It follows, then, that while it is scientifically legitimate and useful to formulate theories of Creation, yet such theories must be based upon well-understood and indisputable facts, or they hardly deserve serious attention. They must also be capable of verification by comparison with other facts. Until the discovery of the four moons of Uranus, it was believed that all the satellites of planets in our system revolved around their primaries from west to east. An explanation of this might have been furnished which should have had all the force and authority of what is usually called a law of nature, but such an explanation would have utterly broken down when it was ascertained that the satellites of Uranus revolved from east to west.

Theories of Creation, no matter under what favourable auspices they may have been advanced, or by how high authorities they are advocated, may yet be destined to perish under the stress of accumulating facts ; unless, indeed, it can be demonstrated that no facts ever could occur which should be inconsistent with them. In many cases it is to be feared that the remarkable words of Goethe are only too accurate an explanation of the way in which hypotheses are begotten and propagated: " Good, intellectual, and courageous heads adorn their minds with such an idea for the sake of its popularity ; they gather followers and pupils, and thus form a literary power ; their idea is finally worked out, exaggerated, and with a passionate impulse is forced upon society." Such theories, however, do not live. They may survive the criticism of a generation or two for want of a full comprehension of their meaning, from a desire to court the influential, or on account of the diffidence of earnest seekers after truth, who forbear to attack what is urged by men of deserved respect until they have tested it in every possible way. But no theory can enjoy immortality that does not continue to bring into line with itself all facts and phenomena with which it has any affinity.

Now, we are brought face to face in Nature with facts whose existence cannot be denied, with phenomena whose recurrence is regular and continuous, with processes or laws which appear at any rate to operate uniformly. The problem as to how these phenomena originated is a totally distinct question from that of their reality. That is to say, the existence of things, the constitution and course of Nature, are accepted by all as realities, while there is an almost endless variety of opinions as to the processes or stages by which these realities came to be what they are. It is usual to describe the stages by which the universe reached its present condition as a Creation. Even Haeckel, at the time when he believed in spontaneous generation, called his great book *The Natural History of Creation.* The method or methods of Creation, which have operated in bringing about the present state of the universe, suggest an altogether distinct idea from that of Creation itself. The moment we begin to make suggestions as to how Creation has proceeded, we leave the region of fact and are starting theories, more or less plausible ; theories which by the ordinary logical and scientific methods establish their right to be regarded as based on uniform laws of nature, or which, under stress of advancing knowledge and improved methods of observation and experiment, may manifest their incompetency and vanish.

From this indisputable fact that the universe exists, we are led on by the logic of necessity to seek for an explanation of its existence. The existence of things implies that they had an original cause. Hume, as is well known, sought to undermine the conception of causality by resolving it into invariable sequence. Positivists regard it as vain to inquire into the causes of phenomena. Many modern scientists, while holding to the universality of causation, yet, with a positivism that even Comte knew nothing of, shut out of the proper field of scientific inquiry the search for all causes that are not physical. The only objects of human knowledge, they are never tired of telling us, are phenomena which may be perceived by the senses, and that everything else is vague, uncertain, transcendental, and can neither be observed nor verified.

This we should readily admit, if by science is meant only material or physical science. But has not science a far wider import? Is it not tautology to say that science is that which deals with what is cognized by the senses, and then to say that what cannot be examined by the senses is not science? It is an altogether arbitrary assumption to say that science has only to do with matter, or with matter and its assumed inherent force. That it is concerned only with matter and force, we need not object to admit; for force is what we call mind and will. Words are poor things at the best, but force which moves, or begets motion, which affects matter, which produces modifications of life and thought,—that surely is mind. It is a mere question of words. But if force be defined so as designedly to exclude mind, then it is not a sufficient or exhaustive classification of things to say that matter and force are all. Even Professor Huxley, in a somewhat jaunty way, but with truth, says : " It seems to me pretty plain that there is a third thing in the universe, to wit, consciousness, which, in the hardness of my heart or head, I cannot see to be matter, or force, or any conceivable modification of either, however intimately the manifestations of the phenomena of consciousness may be connected with the phenomena known as matter and force." (*Fortnightly Review*, December, 1886.)

Whatever philosophers may mean by force, therefore, it seems there is consciousness or mind, for consciousness is mental or nothing. On what ground, then, can we ignore mind, or refuse to admit the validity of its demand for an original cause ?

These attempts to shut out mental phenomena from science and to deride them as belonging to a vain and unprofitable metaphysic are most unscientific. Mind will be heard. Its instincts, intuitions, convictions, cannot be permanently stifled. It knows itself to be greater than matter. It has the consciousness of power, and it postulates in a perfectly scientific manner a Supreme Original, the First Cause of all that is.

The absurdity of excluding from the purview of science all that seems to transcend the senses of man will be seen still more distinctly when

it is remembered that there is no universal agreement as to what senses and sensations are. To
many they involve mind. Here again the Positivist
meets us with the dogmatic declaration that sensation can only be that which is concerned with
material things. Seeing, hearing, and so forth, these
are the only modes of sensation. The cerebral or
nervous modifications, aided by telescope, microscope,
chemical reactions or spectroscopic observations,—
these are the only channels of human knowledge.
But this is just what cannot be made out. The
mind may be conscious of things that stand in no
relation to our material senses. The recent advances in telescopic photography have enabled our
astronomers to prove the existence of celestial
bodies which never have been and perhaps never
may be seen through any telescope. Edison's
phonograph will repeat to generations unborn the
sound of voices never heard by them. Illustrations
are not arguments, of course, but intuition is
certainly a medium of consciousness, it may be
a sensitive plate on which truths are written, a
diaphragm which conveys vibrations to the mind,
that otherwise would not have been brought into
any relation to it.

Such intuitions or convictions, it may be said,
cannot be trusted. Neither can the sight, nor the
ear, nor the brain. Illusions and hallucinations
come to every one. No day passes but we are
reminded that things are not what they seem.
The microscopist has to go through a long ap-
prenticeship before he can interpret aright the

revelations presented in his wondrous instrument, and there are appearances about whose meaning all but the tyro are uncertain. The senses need education, they need constant supervision, and their impressions have frequently to be corrected.

But whatever definition of science may be adopted, it must be admitted by all that Nature cannot be perfectly understood until all her relations are studied, of which the causal relation is one. This must be considered or our science is defective. An efficient Cause of the beginning and continuance of the universe is asked for, and there can never be mental satisfaction or repose till this is found.

We are met with another objection in undertaking this inquiry, and one, as we think, quite as unreasonable as that which we have been combating, notwithstanding that it is urged sometimes by those who are as deeply impressed with the importance of the inquiry as we ourselves. It is said that the question is a theological one, and therefore does not belong to the domain of scientific thought. But it is not exclusively theological. Causality we have shown is a relation of positive existences, it has to do with matter, as well as with life, mind, spirit. It is not purely a problem of metaphysics, still less of theology. If the logical necessities of the case compel us to a belief in God, that does not necessarily imply that the whole subject is a theological one. The fact is, this is a mere device to shelve the question, and mainly on anti-theological grounds. This makes it regrettable that Christian scientists should so easily admit that all such investigations are no legitimate part of science. If to seek for the causes of things is not science, then what is? If one thing more than another has built up modern science into the splendid monument to man's untiring industry and intellectual greatness that it now is, assuredly it is the very fact that men have not been content to remain in ignorance of the causes of things or of any of their inter-relationships. What is gravitation, what are the laws of motion, what is natural selection, but the majestic generalisations of scientific minds, and professedly based upon scientific phenomena or the facts of nature? The sublime generalisation that there is a Deity is a scientific inference, and is the logical consequence of scientific facts. Without that belief nature cannot be explained, the mind of man is unsatisfied. God is a postulate of the scientific mind, and would be conceived even in the absence of the Bible. The existence of God does not belong solely to the supernatural, it is a necessary corollary of the natural. There is a supernatural in theology, but there is a theology which is not outside of the natural. A very weighty sentence from Dr. Dallinger's *Fernley Lecture* emphasizes this : "Science has removed whole regions and æons of phenomena from what was considered the supernatural to the natural ; but to believe that this is so much lost to theology is a feeble and faithless fallacy."

To sum up, then, we hold that the argument for the existence of a Creator falls within the natural as well as the supernatural, for it proceeds

15

along lines laid down by the facts or phenomena of Nature. By demanding an adequate and efficient cause for every effect, science has taught us how to demonstrate, for that is not too strong a word, the existence and even some of the attributes of Deity.

In our time it is not active, dogmatic Atheism in science that the Christian philosopher has to contend with so much as that more negative form of Atheism known by the name of Agnosticism. There are few Atheists now. The name has an unpleasant savour. It is admitted, at length, that the old Psalmist was right in the description he gives of the man who says in his heart, "There is no God." Men accustomed to close reasoning are conscious that so huge a negation cannot be proved. To demonstrate the non-existence of God a man must go everywhere to see, he must question every star and explore limitless space, he must descend into the bowels of the earth and examine all her caverns, he must analyse every atom of the universe and inspect every mode of existence. Till he has done all this he has no right to affirm that there is no God. In some remote system or far-off world, which the most powerful telescope fails to reach, the Deity may sit enthroned in unapproachable splendours ; in some subtle form of essence which no microscope can reveal God may exist ; in some unknown, imperceptible union with all nature, transcending and eluding all human powers of investigation, the Creator may subsist, guiding, sustaining, and delighting in all the works of His hand.

The philosophical Atheist feels the force of these difficulties, and with a prudence that would be admirable did it not raise a suspicion of mental cowardice or prejudice, he adopts the easier method of simply ignoring the whole question. The reality of a primal Cause is not denied, it is declared to be of no importance. The belief in a Creator is superfluous, the universe can be adequately explained without it. But what an impotent conclusion to arrive at, and how unscientific the position of him who reaches it! Here he stands in the midst of order, beauty, life, without seeking any Author of all this. Here are magnitudes compared with which he is a pigmy; here is a mechanism in the presence of whose intricacies he seems a child; around him are forces and energies before which he is helpless; all existing before he came to look upon them, unfading when he dies. Yet he is content to gaze upon all these marvels and never to consider whence they came or how they originated. Is this a scientific attitude to occupy? And yet it is the great boast of Agnosticism that it is scientific. It is astonishing how words can be abused and perverted.

The position of the Agnostic is that of a man who walks through a well-ordered garden, admiring the perfection of the agriculture, delighting in the perfumes and tints of the flowers, refreshing himself with the luscious fruits, and then exclaiming: " I see no evidences here that this place belongs to anybody; I can enjoy all these charms without troubling over the supernatural question as to who is the owner;

I can explain the whole matter without vexing my mind with the transcendental inquiry as to whether this garden has a gardener, these flowers a horticulturalist, these pastures, lawns, and conservatories a proprietor." Such a man would be laughed at or pitied. But if he should go further, and assert that all who did see in the beauty and symmetry around him the traces of originating and presiding intelligence were superstitious or imbecile, then he would become contemptible. He alone is truly scientific who goes beyond the material and seeks to rise through Nature up to Nature's great Original. The search for a new planet suggested by Bode's Law, or by the perturbations of Uranus, was no more rational or scientific than is the belief in a Creator based on Nature's teachings and facts. It is a sober, rational argument, the force of which can be resisted only by the most obstinate prejudice : " Every house is builded by some man; but He that built all things is God " (Heb. iii. 4).

We have endeavoured to argue this question of the existence of a Creator without any detailed reference to what may be regarded as exclusively theological or Biblical. With the intention of using only such evidences as would appeal to those who would not tolerate the importation of Scriptural statement into the discussion, we have passed over many considerations familiar enough to the Christian. It is a distinct gain to us to demonstrate that we have not to rely solely on Revelation for testimony to the existence of Deity, and that such a belief is in line with the strictest philosophy and

the facts of natural science. Even if we have got
no further than to show that the abstract idea of
the Creator's existence is a logical necessity, essential
to the scientific and satisfactory explanation of
Nature, we have placed that doctrine in the same
category with all other great dominant ideas of
science which are accepted as true and immutable,
because, without them, the phenomena which they
account for would remain unexplained. Space, Time,
Gravitation, all the fundamental principles that
underlie astronomy, chemistry, and indeed every
natural science, are abstract ideas, vast inferences;
and yet they are believed in, and regarded as indispensable to the superstructure of doctrine and law
which has been reared upon them. The existence
of a Creator having been shown to be a phase of
the universal law of causality, cannot be disregarded
as being non-scientific. Those who evade the force
of our argument by denying the necessity of an
efficient cause of phenomena and maintaining the
feeble and exploded dogma that causation is mere
sequence, must take the responsibility of explaining
how the first atom began to be, or else of solving
the dense mysteries surrounding the belief in the
eternity of matter.

It follows then from what has been advanced
that what may be called a doctrine of Creation, or
a belief in the fact of Creation, implies a complete
negation of the views of the Materialist, the Atheist,
' the Agnostic, and is an absolute antithesis to
their conception of Nature. To hold any doctrine
of Creation is to accept the existence of a Mind in

Nature, intelligent, supreme, directive, authoritative.
There may be various opinions as to the modes or
laws by which that Supreme Power effected the
origin and development of existing things, but there
cannot be, consistent with a doctrine of creation,
any doubt as to the reality of such a Power. There
may be equal diversity of notions concerning the
essence and character of the Creator, but that He
does exist there is no room to doubt in the case
of those who maintain that a Creation has taken
place.

Now, having cleared out of the way much that
tends to obscure the question, are we in a position
to say what Creation is ; or, to put it in another
form, and one more in harmony with what we have
already said, can we decide how Nature, the sum
and constitution of all material things, came to be
what it is ? Have we any evidence that shall throw
light on the inquiry as to what processes or laws
the Creator adopted in producing the universe, and
bringing it to its present condition ?

Such a question opens up a field of speculation
and investigation far too vast for anything but a
fragmentary treatment here. To give an adequate
answer to it would involve a complete exposition of
all physical and biological science. The principles
and laws which constitute the sciences bearing
on matter and life are in reality the methods of
Creation. Whether they be described as natural
phenomena, the Laws of Nature, physical facts,
or by any other equivalent expression, they are
nothing more nor less than the modes of Creation,

the processes of Divine activity, the expressions and results of the Creator's power.

The simplest and the oldest history of Creation is that which is given in the earlier portion of the Book of Genesis ; the prevalent modern theory of Creation is that which goes by the familiar name of Evolution. Passing by other records or theories, as being of interest only because curious or on account of their being stages in the advance towards the position now held by the majority of scientific men, we wish to fix our attention awhile on these two philosophies.

The question naturally arises, Are they in agreement ; or, if not, which is true ?

It is of course open to the inquirer to ask what is meant by evolution. Materialistic or atheistic evolution, we have already stated, is a conception of Nature with which we are not now dealing. The evolution of Carl Vogt, and the not very different agnosticism of Huxley, Tyndall, and Spencer, are not here taken into consideration ; they require a very different method of treatment, and arguments of quite another sort. What we seek is a clear and distinct definition of Theistic evolution, such as is held by the bulk of scientific men to-day.

Taking Darwin as the most authoritative exponent of evolution, we may regard as a sufficiently accurate idea of it his doctrine of natural selection, involving the emergence of the fittest from the struggle for existence, and under indefinite variations or modifications of structure and environment.

Darwin nowhere affirms the eternity of matter, nor the spontaneous generation of the living out of the non-living, nor the blind, fortuitous action of law. Darwin's theory was concerned in the origin of species, and he begins with the assumption of life.

But creation covers the material or inorganic as well as the living or organic ; and hence we are led on to the nebular hypothesis as a part of modern evolution. La Place taught that the solar system arose from the gradual condensation of a diffused incandescent gas or vapour. Norman Lockyer's recent modification of this is too new and too little considered by the scientific world to make it necessary for us to take it into account. La Place probably wished the inference to be drawn that all other systems or worlds which exist in the remote regions of space were similarly developed. But even he does not show how the primary nebula originated, nor does he demonstrate that the development was anything but the effect of a Supreme Will acting everywhere throughout space. The origin of matter and of force and the beginning of life are vital elements in the case, and are attributed by the majority of evolutionists to the action of some external Power.

With these data, evolutionists start out to explain how Nature came to be what it is. Through all the æons of the geological realm, into all the intricacies of biological science, Darwin travels with a keenness of vision and a strength of intellect almost super-human, and at length arrives at what he considers the universally applicable law of evolution.

And now, without attempting to follow him into
all the details of his vast investigation, and accept-
ing as true all that is involved in the nebular and
evolution hypotheses, can we also give credence
to what we find in Genesis? In a word, are
Creation and Evolution synonymous terms? May
we affirm that what the author of Genesis calls
Creation is practically and in principle the same
thing as Evolution?

In order to answer this question in the affirmative,
we should have to make many demands in regard
to details; we should have to point out that abruptness of change, as well as those gradual modifications
which he postulates, have transpired in the advances
which geological and biological science records,
and especially that mighty upheavals in life and
organization have seemed to occur where ordinary
conditions appear quite inadequate and incommen-
surable. But leaving all this out of consideration,
is there anything in the Mosaic narrative inconsistent with the doctrine that Creation is an
evolution, a process, a law?

The idea, once common, that each star, each
species of plant and animal, was made separately
by a sort of mechanical process, is, we think, quite
obsolete, and deserves to be. It never had a better
foundation than a gross misinterpretation of the
language of Genesis. And although it is to science
that we owe the explosion of the error, now that
it is exploded we wonder it could ever have been
maintained. The utmost that can now be affirmed
with regard to the Mosaic language is that one

of the words used to denote Creation means to produce from nothing, while the other implies to modify what was already in existence. If that be so, it is no more than is required by a rational evolutionist, for he must admit that matter and life were new creations so far as our earth is concerned. We are justified in concluding, therefore, that Creation, as described by the writer of Genesis, means a process or method, or a law, which may as well be called evolution as anything else.

There is, we need hardly say, an extreme school of evolutionists who would demur to our putting of the case. But nothing is easier than to show how they refute themselves. Haeckel, for example, declares that if the primordial cells did not originate spontaneously, they must have been produced supernaturally, an alternative we readily accept, seeing that Haeckel has recently given up the theory of spontaneous generation. Huxley, again, in his article on Biology in the *Encyclopædia Britannica*, says: "If the hypothesis of evolution is true, living matter must have arisen from not living matter: for by the hypothesis the condition of the globe was at one time such, that living matter could not have existed in it, life being entirely incompatible with the gaseous state." And yet in the same article he declares that "at the present moment there is not a shadow of trustworthy direct evidence that abiogenesis (*i.e.*, spontaneous generation) does take place, or has taken place, within the period during which the existence of the globe is recorded."

Such are the inconsistencies and contradictions which the greatest minds are capable of when they seek to bolster up theories at the expense of facts, to maintain evolution without an Evolver, a law without a Lawgiver, a creation without a Creator. But Darwin's evolution is not Huxley's, and, so far as regards its ruling idea, is, we think, not in opposition to the Mosaic narrative,—may, indeed, if we please, be taken as explanatory of it.

It only remains to refer to some minor objections which have been based on the supposed contradictions in Genesis of the facts of geology and some other sciences. These objections mainly bear upon the Mosaic use of the word "day," the order in which the various types of plants and animals were introduced upon the earth, and the antiquity of the human race.

First let me make a brief reference to the bearing of the facts of Geology on the Mosaic "days of Creation."

While men remained ignorant of the marvellous records written upon the stone tablets of the earth, it mattered but little what view was taken with regard to the length of time occupied in Creation ; but when it began to appear that myriads of creatures in all stages of growth and development had been preserved in the rocks, the majority of which no longer exist, then it was suspected that the *yom* of Genesis might mean something different from twenty-four hours. It was felt that six days of twenty-four hours each could not suffice for the growth of many thousands of feet of limestone, chalk, and clay, crowded with the shells and bones of animals which had lived and died. Hugh Miller propounded the theory that the days of Moses corresponded with the geologic periods, and he identified the third, fifth, and sixth days, during which plants and animals were created, with the Primary, or more precisely the Carboniferous, the Secondary, and the Tertiary epochs. Plant life he referred to the Carboniferous, as exemplified in coal; sea-monsters and creeping things characterise the Secondary age, as is seen from the great Saurians of that time; while cattle and beasts are the dominant creatures of the Tertiary period, at the close of which man appeared. This theory has had to be greatly modified under the strain of geological research, but it evidently contains the germ at least of the truth.

Moses himself frequently uses the word *yom* to denote an indefinite period. He does so in the account of the Creation, for he speaks of " the day in which the Lord made the earth and the heavens," and in many other passages of Scripture the same thing occurs. We need not here pursue the argument, for it has already been stated in detail in a former chapter.

As to the order in which the various kinds of plants and animals were introduced upon the earth, the Mosaic narrative does not go into particulars. It merely affirms that first came plants, then fishes, birds, mammals, and man.

It is generally admitted that graphite or plumbago is carbonised vegetable matter, and that iron-ore testifies to plant life. The pre-Cambrian rocks contain deposits of this nature. Again, Moses merely describes the *origin* of things, not their whole after history and development. The first vegetables he calls *deshe*, which signifies lowly plants in general, *i.e.*, seaweeds, lichens, etc.,—in fact, flowerless plants (Cryptogams), which botanists place at the bottom of the scale. Herbs yielding seed, and trees bearing fruit, the higher botanical division of Phanerogams or flowering plants, appeared in later times, when the earth's condition had become more favourable to their survival.

On the fifth day Moses says that "the waters brought forth the moving creatures," or *sheretzim*, a word which in Leviticus xi. is applied to insects, creeping things, and small creatures generally. The proper word for "fish" does not occur till verse twenty-six, which refers to man's dominion over terrestrial things. The word *sheretzim*, then, probably refers to lowly marine life and insects, many of which pass their larval condition in water. No better word than *tanninim* could have been used by which to denote the great sea-monsters of the Secondaries, and so Moses, like the geologist, puts reptiles before birds. With regard to the higher class of mammalia there is no dispute. Nothing can be clearer, therefore, than that the writer of Genesis, when interpreted correctly, is in perfect accord with the demonstrated facts of Geology.

The subject of man's antiquity is a vast one, and can only be alluded to briefly. The whole point of the objection turns upon the rate at which certain deposits in which human relics are found were laid. The geological chronometer is itself so unreliable that apparent discrepancies between its indications and the statements of Moses need cause but little concern. Scripture chronology is also a very complex problem, and there is room for very great differences of opinion in regard to the age of man. We require to know a great deal more about the conditions of stratification in primeval times, and we also need more accurate methods of determining the dates of Biblical events, before any final judgment can be arrived at as to whether or not there is any inconsistency between the Scripture history and Geology on the subject of man's antiquity.

But now, reverting to the main question of this chapter, although we have endeavoured to show that Creation and Evolution may be synonymous terms, and that there is nothing in the Mosaic narrative inconsistent with the idea of a progressive creation by process or law, yet we are not therefore bound to believe that the prevalent views concerning evolution are true. There is much in Nature to show that evolution has a good deal of truth in it; but not even its adherents claim that it contains the whole truth. Indeed, the theory is undergoing constant criticism and modification at the hands of scientific experts. There is much to be investigated yet before any complete and final scheme can be systematized which shall give a full account of all the laws of development. When Science has finished its "Genesis," if ever that day should arrive, it will be time enough to consider what its relationship is to the Genesis of the Bible. And if it should turn out that Creation is Evolution, there will be no shock sustained by the venerable beliefs of those who maintain that "the heavens declare the glory of God, and the firmament showeth His handiwork."

> "His parent Hand
> From the mute shell-fish gasping on the shore
> To men, to angels, to celestial minds,
> For ever leads the generations on
> To higher scenes of being; while, supplied
> From day to day with His enlivening breath,
> Inferior orders in succession rise
> To fill the void below."

XVI.

THE MINISTRY OF NATURE.

"To him who in the love of Nature holds
Communion with her visible forms, she speaks
A various language."

BRYANT.

AS Nature any ministry higher than that which seeks man's material welfare? Has she any revelations of her Author to make, to us, or can she throw any light, however feeble, upon our relationship to God? In the principles of the Divine government, in the processes of God's providence, in the working out of His vast purpose to make all sentient beings happy, in our Heavenly Father's plan for the redemption of the human race, is there room, or is there need, for Nature's teaching? Those who interpret the phenomena and laws of the universe, can they peaks to men on these vast themes with words that are intelligible enough to be understood and wise enough to be accepted?

The human conscience needs all the light it can get wherewith to make the path of duty clearer;

the heart of man, under its mighty burdens of sorrow, is thankful for every alleviation of its anguish ; the immortal spirit within us eagerly throws out its tendrils of love and trust in search of whatever promises to bear it up into a healthier, diviner air. What is there for us to read in this wonderful many-paged volume, which lies wide open and inviting everywhere around us, that shall illumine the conscience and guide the judgment, that shall give fortitude to stricken hearts and inspiration to labouring souls ?

To the devout and thoughtful, Nature has much to say concerning God and duty and immortality. It is worth while to pause, now and then, and listen to this many-tongued preacher that discourses with such sweet and varied eloquence upon the deep problems of life and eternity.

Some there are, no doubt, to whom our invocation is vain babbling. Their mind being at enmity against God, all revelations of God, of which Nature is one, are but as the shining of the sun to the weak-eyed owl or the feeble-winged bat ; but there are others to whom the universe is ablaze with the glory which awed Moses in the presence of the burning bush. Frigid and unspiritual men there are who view everything around them in the beam of dry light which originates from the human intellect, and who discover only physical facts or inexorable laws or unmeaning and incalculable contingencies ; but the best and wisest scholars in Nature's school are those who discern in creation the footsteps of a Creator, and see in the works of

16

the Lord the irradiation of His wisdom and love.
Such as these

    " Find tongues in trees, books in the running brooks,
    Sermons in stones, and good in every thing."

What we wish to do, then, in this chapter, is to
claim for Science that its highest function is to display the presence and operations of God in the
natural world : " The works of the Lord are great,
sought out of all them that have pleasure therein."

I. And what a pleasure this is which Nature
offers to the devout and spiritual ! It is the rapture
which was experienced in Eden, and it is among
the purest of our gratifications ; it is given to the
poor and the rich. This starry sky, this flower-
bedecked earth, this grove ringing with the songs
of birds, are all ours without purchase and without
rent. How vain are sensual delights, ending in
weariness and disgust, compared with the lofty
pleasures of the reason and the soul which the
contemplation of God's great works inspires ! Mr.
Frederic Harrison, the apostle of Positivism, has
declared that raptures are out of place where religion
is concerned, for they disturb the intellectual vision ;
yet the soul that never mounts up " with wings as
eagles " is not likely to run without weariness or
walk without fainting on the difficult path of duty.

The pleasure we derive from devout contemplation
of God's works is not such as to pamper conceit or
pride, but it tends to deepen our reverence for all
that is Divine, and cultivates humility ; as Lord
Bacon said : " The kingdom of men found in science

is like the kingdom of God. It can be entered only
in the character of a little child." The tiniest insect
has problems connected with its vital functions
which the greatest minds have not been able to
solve. Who can explain how the thousands of
minute lenses which make up the eyes of the dragon-
fly flash but one image along their numerous nerves
to the centre of sensation ? What man has ever
explained how it is that the suspended vitality of
the chrysalis, so far from ending in death, does but
prepare it for the more glorious life of the butterfly
which bursts forth from the clod to roam through
the garden and the glade ? Those myriads of
systems which the telescope discovers, those busy
worlds in atoms which the microscope reveals ; who
is able to compass the majestic meaning or penetrate
into all the profound mysteries which are here
involved ?

This pleasure, moreover, refines and ennobles
man ; for only to look upon the beauty which glad-
dens him in all the diversity of hill and vale, of
gleaming river and ocean, of radiant garden and
many-coloured forest, of sparkling sunlight and
lustrous cloud, of peaceful evening and starry night,
brings a consciousness of nobility. And when
we "look through Nature up to Nature's God,"
how calm and trustful do intelligent Christians
become, and with what ardour they awake all their
powers to praise that beneficent Being to Whom we
owe all these possessions and delights ! A puny
soul has he who never feels inspired to glorify our
Heavenly Father Who has placed us amid this

scene of magnificence, where all things are conducive
to our highest welfare. Not upon some gigantic
cinder, as the moon is said to be, porous with the
vents and craters left by desolating fires as the
evidence of their dreadful forces, now gaping for
showers and dew that can never come out of an arid
sky ; but in a veritable Paradise—though slimed
with the trail of sin—has God placed His children of
the earth. And they who are wise enough to contemplate the Divine benevolence in Nature's laws
and arrangements do themselves become more like
God, and realise a foretaste of that "fulness of joy,"
which, we may hope, will be ours when our knowledge of God's works shall no longer be incomplete,
but we shall "know even as also" we are "known."

Are we not right, then, in saying that to bring to
man the delight of communion with God in Nature
is the highest function of science ?   The truest glory
of a painting does not lie in the pigments that cover
the canvas, but in its power to speak as from the
soul of the artist to the soul of him who admires
the thought of which the picture is the embodiment.
And while it is good to admire scientific method
and natural law, it is better to worship the Mind
which that method discloses, and which made that
law. Thus are we touched at our noblest points,
and our truest humanity is awakened to sublime
soarings of thought and instinctive yearnings for
holiness.

II. The suggestion is common in these days that
the proper domain of science is the positive or
material, and that Nature ought to be studied apart

from any consideration of the supernatural. But
Nature and the supernatural cannot be separated by
any clear-cut line of distinction. Paradoxical as the
assertion may seem, they are one. Who can possibly
examine the lowest vegetable forms, the diatoms,
whose elaborate and delicate tracery, as delineated
in the microscope, no weaver's skill could rival, and
yet not ask what wondrous Artificer moulded and
fashioned them, and decorated the marge of the
stagnant pond or the rocky ocean-pool with such
perfect though minute beauties of structure, thus
gratifying the vision as well as satisfying the wants
of those tiny creatures whose food they mainly
constitute? And how could any intelligent being
watch the Protean transformations of the lowest
animal organisms, the Amœbæ, whose pseudo-fingers
shoot forth from every part of them when they
desire to grasp their prey, and are drawn back into
the slimy substance of the creature as soon as
its victim has been absorbed, without being led to
wonder from what Source of life these vital functions
were derived? But questions like these involve
the introduction of the supernatural, and hence
Nature cannot even be observed properly without
quitting the narrow shore of visible fact for the
boundless sea of the Divine. Every line of investigation along which the scientist proceeds must lead
him sooner or later to inquire concerning the supreme
First Cause of all that is ; and if at that point these
questionings of the intellect are stifled by the answer
that they are beyond the province of the student
of Nature, then assuredly the mind is degraded, its

most splendid powers are paralyzed, and its crown
is thrown recklessly into the dust. Great and ador-
able Creator! can that reason with which Thou hast
endowed us as the glory of our being be put to nobler
exercise than to search for the vestiges of Thy greatness and wisdom in the things which sprang from
Thy creative energy, and are sustained by Thine
unceasing benevolence ?

Yet there are those who, " professing to be wise,
become fools ; " and, failing to perceive, " through
the things that are made, His everlasting power
and Godhead," glorify not God, and even gloat over
the belief that He is at length banished out of His
own universe. But when we recollect that the
belief in God has constituted the brightest hope of
the sad and wearied of all generations, that it has
quenched the violence of martyrs' fires and inspired
timid women and even children to die rather than
offend their conscience or disobey the sacred voice
of duty, that it has restrained the natural passions
of the most sensual, and fanned in them the
flickering desire for a holier character and life,
—what words but those of fervent indignation can
we utter against those who would teach us all to
say : " There is no God " ?

The man who is possessed of every comfort,
and is surrounded by tender friends who watch
solicitously for his safety and hasten to anticipate
his slightest want, and who should yet with his
own rash hand apply to his beautiful home the
torch that shall burn it down and destroy the lives
of those who are devoted to him, would rightly be

judged a madman ; and surely it can be called nothing but moral insanity when men set themselves to expel from human beliefs the doctrine of a loving Father Whose compassion for His creatures is boundless, and Whose resources of grace for our security from sin and misery are infinite. Wherever the knowledge of God has been cast off, moral degradation has been the result, and the human heart has sunk under the fearful conception of irresistible destiny.

Not that we need fear that the world will ever come to this. The consolations that spring from trust in God in hours of woe and perplexity are too many and too precious to be given up at the bidding of a dreary Materialism. Many a dreaded rival of Christianity, assuming the garb of truth or philanthropy, has been found to contain nothing but the marsh-born elements of an intellectual *ignis fatuus ;* a very slight examination has sufficed to detect in it the exhalations of stagnant error and a degraded moral life ; while this venerable belief in a good, wise God has a firmer hold upon the conscience and the heart of men to-day than ever it had. " They are dead which sought the Child's life ; " the Child has continued to grow "in stature, . . . and in favour with . . . man."

III. But there is another and a worse error against which we must be upon our guard—the notion that Nature is by itself a sufficient revelation of God. Nature cannot answer all the questionings of the human spirit, nor can the perturbations of the conscience and the heart be lulled to rest by any

response which science has to give. These hiero-
glyphics that are stamped on the page of creation
are not easy to decipher, and even those who spend
their whole time and strength in the study of them
spell out the words but slowly, and are often in
doubt as to what they mean. Vague and Sphinx-
like at the best are the answers which are returned
to the grave and anxious inquiries of thoughtful
men by the great Oracle that is enshrined in the
material universe. Of Law it speaks, but gives no
help to those who fain would obey ; of suffering it
tells, yet reveals its alleviations and remedies but
slowly ; of death it prophesies, but gives no promise
of immortality. To a few cultivated children of
genius it has something to say, but to the mass of
helpless seekers after happiness it is dumb. It
discloses truth to the patient student, but not all
the truth, nor yet the highest truth. Its light is
the trembling glimmer of a star, not the radiance
of the sun ; nay, it is like some dim and remote
nebula, invisible even through the astronomer's
telescope, and whose existence can only be shown
from the faint rays which are caught upon the
highly-sensitized plate of the photographer. We
need a distincter voice and a clearer light than
Nature owns, if we are to find our way to the
Temple of Truth. This voice we have ; this light
gilds our path. "God hath at the end of these
days spoken unto us in His Son ;" He " hath shined
in our hearts to give the light of the knowledge of
the glory of God in the face of Jesus Christ."

IV. From the foregoing considerations it follows

that Science is most worthily pursued when our
aims are in harmony with the Scriptures, and
our investigations transfigured and controlled by
reverence for true religion. This involves no
sacrifice of freedom in the use of our intellectual
powers, nor will it produce mental stagnation or
paralysis by imposing unnatural restraints or de-
grading limitations upon thought. That so-called
free-thought, the temerity of which is its only
excellence, and which is displayed chiefly in un-
provoked assaults upon whatsoever is holy and
venerable, is more remarkable for its freedom than
for its thoughtfulness. All thought that deserves
the name has its necessary laws, to offend against
which is unsafe. If the processes of reasoning
have to be conducted in harmony with certain
forms of thought, it is not inconsistent with true
intellectual freedom to carry on the study of nature
along those lines which are laid down in the Sacred
Volume, the evidences of whose Divine origin and
authority are so numerous and overwhelming. The
proper aim of science is to establish truth upon
secure foundations, not to buttress fascinating
theories. When men of science, therefore, permit
themselves to revel in mere speculations that they
know to be unfriendly to religion, they leave their
rightful sphere and violate the laws of thought.
The scientific method of seeking truth is not the
bending of facts to upset what has already been
sufficiently demonstrated, but it is the observation
of phenomena for the purpose of inferring new
generalizations. For example, the naturalist who

inquires into the principles of animal and vegetable growth, begins by examining individual plants and animals, observing their transformations of structure, and noting the modes of their development and reproduction. The conclusions he draws from such investigations are not at once accepted, but he proceeds to verify them by other instances, until at length he reaches a position which is assailed by no fact so far as he knows, and then he believes he has discovered a scientific truth or law. Now, there are moral and spiritual phenomena which demonstrate the cardinal truths of Christianity quite as conclusively as natural and physical facts establish the laws of nature. They, therefore, are as truly scientific who by means of a clear and philosophic method seek to explain the facts of Christian experience or consciousness, the problems of duty, of moral responsibility and spiritual life, as are those who confine their investigations to material things ; and consequently the principles and beliefs of the former cannot be ignored or contemned by any who pretend to maintain a scientific attitude.

V. We are far from affirming that positive science ought not to inquire into facts that may seem to be unfriendly to some cherished Christian beliefs. All we urge is that mere theories unsubstantiated by evidence shall not be brandished against the Scriptures rightly interpreted. It is well both for science and faith that everything in nature, whatever may be its apparent bearing upon religion, should be thoroughly investigated. Only thus can science be

freed from error, and false interpretations of the
Scriptures be superseded. The history of science
records the overthrow of many a false and anti-
religious notion as the result of continued and more
accurate examination. An instance of this sort is
presented by the theory of spontaneous generation.
Haeckel, one of the most laborious of scientific men,
albeit somewhat speculative, bent his strength to
the task of demonstrating that the non-living
became by its own inherent qualities a living
organism ; and Professor Huxley went so far as
to suggest that the ooze dredged up from the deep
sea-bottom was the identical protoplasm on its way
from death to life, calling the substance, in honour
of his continental collaborateur, *Bathybius Haeckelii.*
Strauss at once took hold of these speculations and
used them against the Christian faith. Recent experiments, however, have shown that the theory of
spontaneous generation has not a single fact to rest
upon, and Professor Huxley now laughs at his
former error, while even Haeckel has materially
modified his opinions. This shows the value both
to religion and science of earnest, serious efforts to
discover truth in every direction.

There are other theories before the world just
now which have provoked the opposition of a large
number of intelligent Christians on the ground that
they militate against the teaching of the Bible.
Some of these hypotheses bear upon the development of living things and the origin of man. We
may be sure, however, that the same course will be
pursued in these cases as in those already referred

to. Some are unwisely imitating the example of
Strauss, and they will experience a similar dis-
comfiture. The evolution theory will be tried by all
the facts that men of science are now assiduously
collecting, and if it fail to fit in with those facts, it
will have to give way to some better doctrine ; but
if it should be shown to present a satisfactory interpretation of *all* the conditions involved, it will of
course take its place among the laws of nature ;
and Christianity will no more suffer from the establishment of a true theory of Creation than it
did from the establishment of the truth in regard to the earth's revolution by Copernicus and
Galileo. But it is too soon to be flourishing so
incomplete an hypothesis as that of Darwin as
an argument against the immediate agency of
God in creation, especially as there are *forms*
of evolution which are held by many prominent
Christian scientists.

Of true science, cultivated in the spirit for which
we contend, the Christian need have no fear. If
a few unimportant dogmas, whose only claim to
acceptance is that they were pronounced *ex cathedra*,
have not been able to survive the test of scientific
progress, then they deserved to die. Theological
statements which threaten to smother the truth
they were intended to protect are sure to perish
before advancing knowledge, and no one is poorer
for the loss. It is the glory of real science that
it fearlessly pushes aside all preconceived ideas ;
and, like the huge beast of the forest or jungle,
which tramples under foot the tangled brushwood

which bars its way, makes a clear path through error and confusion into the open spaces of truth.

VI. Even in regard to our study of the Scriptures, we owe much to the friendly offices of science. The Bible is inspired, but not so all its readers ; and the most diligent among these will be the readiest to admit that with regard to Biblical criticism, grammar, and rhetoric, the customs of the times in which the various books of Scripture were written, and the state of knowledge to which the peoples had attained who first received those books, the researches of Christian scientists have been of the utmost value. The old-world forms of speech which the inspired writers used as their vernacular, and as the only expressions which would be understood by the men of their times, need to be transfused with the fuller knowledge which we now possess. There is a wide distinction between the real significance of a word or doctrine and its human interpretation ; hence there are passages of Scripture in which there lies a divinely-born truth, perfect and unchanging in its essence, but presented to the mind of man under varying forms in successive ages, just as the beautiful water-insect is unchanged in form although its outline appears distorted from the refraction of the rays of light which make it visible. No one now thinks that the Bible teaches us to believe in the existence of a metal *firmament* around the confines of our atmosphere. Here, and in many other instances, we owe it to science that now we have truer and more beautiful interpretations of the Scriptural terms which at one time seemed to favour false views.

Moreover, there are innumerable lessons of importance in God's Word that must have for ever lain hid but for the vigilance and industry of men of science. "There are two books," said Sir Thomas Browne, "from which I collect my divinity; besides that written one of God, there is another of His servant Nature—that universal and public manuscript which lies expansed unto the eyes of all."

Take the passage already quoted, "The works of the Lord are great," and consider how much scientific researches have done to flood it with a meaning it could never have had if men had not deeply studied "the works of the Lord." What rich treasures of thought are opened, what genuine admiration of God's power and skill is awakened in the soul, as we contemplate the wonders of sky and earth and sea, the beauties of form, and the inexpressible adaptation of life to environment, in the light shed upon Nature by the lamp of the Christian philosopher!

Again, when we remember what modern physiology and anatomy have taught us concerning the marvels of the human body, the admirable adjustments of bones and joints so as to secure the greatest strength with the least weight, the elaborate arrangements for the digestion and assimilation of food, the intricate methods by which the various secretions are collected in the glands, or, if injurious, ejected from the system; the perfect machinery by which the blood, the current

of life, is purified, and conveys by means of its
corpuscles the necessary oxygen to every part of
our frame, while the carbonic acid is carried back
to the lungs and exhaled; and, above all, the
exquisite organisation of the nerves and brain,
connecting in some secret, subtle manner, which
has eluded all man's efforts to discover it, the
sentient, thinking soul with the external world,—
how much more expressive and intelligent does
the old cry become : " l will praise Thee ; for I am
fearfully and wonderfully made."

Once more, we may point to recent meteorology
as helping the devout soul to enter into sympathy
with the ecstatic outburst of the Psalmist : " Thy
mercy, O Lord, is in the heavens ; and Thy faith-
fulness reacheth unto the clouds!! " There also,
where all seems confusion, law prevails ; there,
where lurid storms breed, mercy reigns. The
mildest colours and the most beautiful hues meet
the eye as we look into the slumbering purple of
heaven's vault ; the sun's fierce heat and dazzling
brilliance are tempered by soft, fleecy clouds which
float with fairy form before his face ; the most
marvellous arrangements are continually being
discovered for the distribution of the fertilising
dew and refreshing rain over the thirsty earth, as
well as for the removal from the atmosphere of
those poisonous gases and fluids which would prove
destructive to living things.

Thus does science carry on its divine ministry
in man's behalf. In a myriad ways it illumines
and emphasises the testimony of the written Word

to the greatness of God's works; it adds to the
sum of human happiness by unlocking treasures
of thought and beauties of. form which might
otherwise have remained for ever hid; it teaches
us to discern the sources and nature of many ills,
and lays at our feet alleviations and remedies; it
redeems the pure Word of Life from the obscura-
tions caused by the poverty or the falsity of human
interpretations; and, above all, it purifies and
ennobles man's spirit by leading him into communion with his Maker, humbling him before the
unfolded magnificence of nature, evoking his grati-
tude in the presence of that Divine benevolence
which characterises all creation, and begetting in
his heart deep longings for that complete and
restful harmony with God's laws which suffuses
the whole universe with sweet and hallowed peace,
the outshining of God's own blessedness, to contemplate which inspires the soul to exclaim—

> "Thine this universal frame
> Thus wondrous fair; Thyself how wondrous then!"

Printed by Hazell, Watson, & Viney, Ld., London and Aylesbury

www.ingramcontent.com/pod-product-compliance
Lightning Source LLC
Chambersburg PA
CBHW031423020726
47499CB00005B/1570